# A Side Lake Summer

## JENNIFER WALTERS

To Mel ~
Thank you for reading!

*[signature]*

Also By Jennifer Walters

**The Fredrickson's Series**

Always Right Here

Northern Winds

Greenrock Road

**TURTLE CREEK SERIES**

The Memories We Keep

A Side Lake Summer

**Standalone**

The Weight of Change

*To Brelyn, my childhood best friend,*
*and the rest of the Kritz family.*
*For all the summers*
*spent at your family cabin in Side Lake*
*making memories I will cherish forever.*

*In memory of Maria Kritz,*
*1953-2023*

*Now*

Four sheriff cars were parked out front when I opened my door and threw my bag over my shoulder. My face flushed and my hands shook as I approached two deputies standing on the sidewalk. Two small boys who could not be older than five sat at their feet, drawing with sidewalk chalk.

Before I said hello, a familiar face took a few steps in my direction. His eyes captivated me, and made it impossible for me to look away.

"The drug task force is inside. They found meth pipes, a scale, ten pounds of white substance Ms. Kline admitted was methamphetamines, and close to five thousand dollars in cash. We're waiting for your direction on what to do with the kids."

I threw my shoulders back and stood up a little taller. I was instantly lost in his eyes. A shiver ran down my spine. He stared back at me with a blank look. It was Kevin Finney. Not even an ounce of recognition on his face. He was my best friend as a teenager and my first crush. I knew we would be crossing paths eventually, but I hated that it happened today. It hurt he had no reaction at all.

· · ·

Was it possible he was taller than the last time I saw him? He was stockier and even more confident than he was ten years ago, and his jawline was stronger and more defined. He was even more handsome than I remembered. Just seeing him made my heart beat faster.

"I see two kids out here, but she has three, right? A little girl, too?"

"Talk to Deputy Hill, he's in charge."

He was talking at me instead of to me.

"He must be inside?"

He nodded.

I pointed to the boys, who did not seem fazed by all of this. "Are they okay with you guys for a minute while I check it all out?"

He nodded his head and turned away. Did he really hate looking at me that much? His short sleeves showed off his bulging muscles. How hadn't he ripped his uniform yet when he moved his arms?

I walked inside the home with a quick knock to alert those inside of my presence. An officer greeted me at the door, obviously on high alert. Magazines, newspapers, garbage, and miscellaneous items were piled high in the front room. The end tables were stacked with boxes and garbage, and the floor was covered in clothes, car batteries, drain cleaner, and frozen dinner boxes and wrapper garbage. An ashtray lay upside down on the floor and a scattered trail of butts led to the next room. And the smell ... what was that smell? Feces mixed with moldy food? I put my finger to my nose to block it out.

"Hi, Lyndsey, I heard you were a social worker now."

Lance was the head of the drug task force. He had yet to age from the last time I saw him, about fifteen years ago in law enforcement school.

"Yeah, for a couple months now. Where are the mother and the little girl?"

"In the kitchen."

We chatted for a minute or two, then he led me into the kitchen. Moldy food covered the counters, the sink overflowed with dirty dishes, which were also stacked on the cupboard by the sink. Trash and clothes lined the floors. The room looked as if someone opened a garbage bag and dumped it all over the floor. Only the garbage can was full, too.

I had to watch the ground with each step to make sure I didn't step on anything that might shatter or smoosh beneath my feet. Random stuffed animals and baby toys were stacked in piles, ready to topple over if bumped slightly. I could hardly find the kitchen table under all the junk.

A woman sat at what looked to be the table, her head in her hands. Her sobbing turned hysterical when she saw me.

"You must be Kelly." I reached for the chair next to her, but food was smudged into the cushion, so I decided standing was my best option.

She looked up at me and wiped away her tears. "You're here to take my babies, aren't you?" Her eyes were black, and her hands shook.

A little girl was wrapped around her legs. I did not see her at first because she blended in with all the random stuff around her. She had blonde hair knotted in matts and grease and bright blue eyes.

I crouched down, careful not to let my knees touch the dirty floor. "Hi, sweetie, what's your name?"

She hid her head in between her mother's legs.

Kelly cried harder. "Please don't take my babies."

Great way to scare a child and make this situation worse than it already was.

The little girl dug her nails into her head, scratching with such force it sent chills down my spine. Was it lice or dry skin? Bed bugs? I'd seen it all, and I'd caught lice three times this year already, but the risks did not stop me from doing my job.

"Do you have a friend or relative they could stay with for a couple days?"

She picked up the little girl, who was now crying in response to her mother's sobs and hysteria. She held the little girl tight to her chest. "She's trying to take you away from me." Her eyes lifted to meet mine. "How can you take them away from their mother? I didn't do anything wrong. I didn't even know the drugs were here. Someone must have hid them in my house."

I looked at Lance and he stared blankly at me. My job was to take the lead now, but my hands shook. The woman was not going to make this easy for me or her children.

"Kelly, let's call someone. Who do you trust to pick them up?"

I hated that I had to have this conversation with her in front of the little girl. I could not imagine how traumatizing this was for a four-year-old to see, to live in.

Kelly stared in silence without answering me. Was she high or just trying to think?

"It would be best for your children to go with someone they trust so you can get help."

The little girl turned her head in my direction and held onto her mother tighter. She let out a loud cry.

"We need to continue this conversation, but not in front of her," I said in a whisper. "There is no reason for her to hear this."

The little girl pulled on her mother's shirt. Her neckline stretched with the tug. Kelly stood up and roughly pulled her daughter's hands off her. The little girl fell back and landed in a pile of dirty clothes and garbage on the floor. Kelly had no reaction to her daughter falling. Nor did she reach out and grab her. She just looked away.

The deputy opened his hand, revealing a purple iPhone. She snatched the phone from his hand in one quick swoop.

"Keep the phone where we can see it and put it on speaker phone," he said.

Even I felt a bit intimidated by his tone.

"Hello," a voice said on the other line.

"Moooom!" Kelly's voice came out as a loud, screechy cry.

"What's wrong?"

"Can you pick up the kids? Child protection is here threatening me."

"Again, Kelly? What did you do now?"

"Nothing! They're harassing me!"

I put my hand on the little girl's back. She had heard enough. "Should we go see what your brothers are doing outside?"

She jumped to her feet like I had just slapped her and ran to the door, tripping and falling over another pile of junk stacked in her way. She got up without a peep and ran out the door. I followed closely behind her. The bright sun blinded my view as I stepped onto the front porch. I blinked away my tears.

"You got her?" I said to no deputy in particular and one of them nodded but looked annoyed. "The grandmother may be here in a few minutes. I need to do a background check on her first."

I pulled a file out of my bag and approached Kelly. I sent a text to my co-worker back at the office to get the background check started.

I placed a paper and pen on the table. "These are our privacy practices—"

"I've been through this before. Too many times. All you guys care about is paperwork. Can't you just save the old stuff?" She grabbed the papers from me and signed them, throwing the pen back on the table.

I tore open a packaged urinalysis and placed it on the table in front of her. Before I had a chance to say anything, she grabbed the cup and stomped her way to the bathroom. I followed her and pulled on gloves.

"What will show positive in your urine?"

"Nothing. Although, I think my boyfriend put some meth in my coffee, but I haven't used, I swear."

Same familiar story I'd heard far too many times.

"Are you going to watch me pee? You have nothing better to do with your life or what?"

"I need to observe so we know it's your urine."

"Who the hell's urine would I be using? No one else is here. You're all the same stupid social workers, I swear."

Her UA was positive for methamphetamines, amphetamines, THC (marijuana), and PCP.

"Since you're positive, your kids will need to stay with your mom for a while. You have a few options here. I have a Voluntary Placement Agreement you can sign so your kids can go with your mother right away."

She crossed her arms around her waist. "What happens if I refuse to sign it?"

"Then I would have to get a police hold, hold an emergency pre-petition screening, and go before the court. You might get arrested today. My job is to make sure your children are safe and they aren't safe here, right now. I promise that if you want your kids to come home, I will do everything I can to help you. You just have to be willing to put in the work."

She looked down. "What kind of work would I need to be doing exactly?"

"First, you need a Substance Use Assessment set up at a treatment center of your choice. If they recommend you go into treatment, then you need to go into treatment. You need to be honest, and it isn't going to be easy, but you will have to take it one day at a time. What do you say?"

She put her head in her hands and cried.

"Kelly, we will get through this together, okay? I'm on your side. Your kids need you, but you can't be a mom until you focus on you first. They need a healthy mother."

She nodded then shook her head and rolled her eyes. She signed the paperwork.

"You need to clean your house. This isn't a safe place for your kids right now. Do you have a friend or family member who can help you?"

She nodded. "My friend, Olivia, I guess."

"Is she sober?"

"Yes."

"Okay, I'll see if your mom is outside now. Her background came back clear. I will come back in a couple of days if you aren't in jail. But you need to get the Chemical Assessment completed either in jail or at a treatment facility right away, okay?"

She stared ahead blankly.

I tried to build her up and give her hope. I knew the chances were good she would get her kids back, but not until she was sober.

The grandmother was already out front, and the kids were standing with her next to the car. My favorite deputy, Kevin Finney, was standing right there next to them.

"Hi, Ida. Why don't we get the kids in the car and then you and I can have a quick talk."

Once the kids were in the car, their grandma forced a smile my way as she rubbed the back of her neck.

"Kelly is really struggling right now with drugs. Due to the suspected meth use in the home, we will not be able to send any clothes or toys with the kids. Do you have anything for them at your house?"

She nodded. "Yeah, I have some clothes, but not a lot. They should last a few days. I just worry about the little ones not having their favorite toys."

"Well, if there's anything you need, please let me know. If it gets to be too much, let me know. Kelly is not to have any contact with the children. If she shows up at your house demanding her kids back, you need to call 9-1-1. Can you do that? I know it isn't easy when it's your daughter."

Her eyes began to water. "No, I can do it if I need to."

"She may be going to jail, but I'm not sure what is happening right now. Look on the county jail roster if you're concerned."

"I can't believe this is happening again. Kelly's father and I never used drugs."

"It's not your fault. They are really lucky to have you here to help." I handed her some paperwork to fill out, including her contact information. She handed it back to me and I gave her my card.

"Call me if you have any questions, okay? You aren't alone. I'm here to help."

"Thank you."

She closed her car door and took off down the road.

Deputy Finney and I stood alone in front of the house. Awkward.

I cleared my throat. "Thank you for all your help today. I know watching these kids isn't your job, but I didn't want them sitting in the house listening to everything going on."

He still did not look at me. Instead, he stared straight ahead as he answered. "I've been doing this for many years, I'm not afraid to help out when needed. It's my job."

I found it hard to believe he was once my very best friend in the world.

He turned around and climbed into his police car without another word. I'd be lying if I said it didn't hurt.

## Then

The Finneys moved into the cabin next door to my house on Turtle Creek Road when I was sixteen. Mr. and Mrs. Finney were doctors, and Kevin and his brother spent a lot of time at the cabin by themselves. They only lived there in the summer.

Their four-bedroom cabin was bigger than my house next door. It looked more like a house than a cabin. The house had a beautiful deck overlooking West Sturgeon, just like ours but nicer and bigger.

I will never forget the first time I saw Kevin Finney. I was sitting at the end of my dock, and I looked over to find him taking off his shirt. He was thin and tall, and he had the most gorgeous brown hair. I could not help but stare. As a teenage girl, I swooned over his half naked body.

He put on a life jacket and got into his kayak. I was pretty sure he did not see me but then my stupid brother came running at me. His footsteps creaked over the old wooden dock with each step, the noise echoing off the lake.

I saw Kevin grin out of the corner of my eye. He knew I had no way to escape from my brother. No matter what, I was going in, so I jumped into the water fully dressed before my brother reached me.

Brad stopped and stared at me, his arms crossed.

"Don't you know there's such a thing called a swimming suit?" He laughed at his own joke.

I splashed him, and he jumped back.

"Unlike you, I would like to get my trunks on before I jump into the lake." He headed up the dock in the direction of our house.

I looked over at the kayak and caught Kevin staring at me. He waved and muffled his laugh by putting a fist in front of his mouth. I pulled my hand out of the water and waved back, my smile smug. He kept paddling, but he turned his head to look back at me again and caught me staring.

Heat bloomed across my face, spreading to my core like wildfire. I turned away and swam to shore, pretending I did not know he was watching me.

The next day was the hottest day of summer so far. I sat on the edge of my dock, my feet dangling in the water while I read a book. I heard footsteps behind me, so I peeked over my shoulder to find my hot neighbor heading my way. I turned back around, and he sat down next to me.

He took the book from my hands. "What are you reading?"

I grabbed my book back and hid it out of his reach. "Who do you think you are and why are you here?"

"I wanted to see what book could be so good that you aren't swimming on such a hot day."

"You wouldn't understand."

"Try me."

"Let me guess, you're too cool to read?"

He crossed his arms and scooted even closer to me. "As a matter of fact, I read John Grisham."

"John Grisham? Let me guess, you want to be a lawyer when you grow up?"

He laughed. I loved the way the vein on his forehead stuck out when he laughed.

"No. A police officer."

"Oh." Now that he said that it did not surprise me given his confident demeanor. I always looked up to police officers. They had an immense responsibility and when everyone was scared and running out of their houses due to danger, police officers were running in. I grew up with my father being a police officer, so law enforcement was my normal.

He examined my book from an arm's length. "Is it romance?"

"No, nosy. Do I look like a romance reader to you? I hate romance books. They're so cheesy. I like mysteries."

He put his sunglasses on the top of his head, and his beautiful blue eyes stared back at me. I wished I had sunglasses to hide my surprised gaze.

"Mary Higgins Clark?"

I put my nose back in my book. "Yes, brainiac." No way was I letting him see the effect he had on me when our eyes met.

"There is a time and place for that, and this beautiful day is not it." He pulled on my arm.

"Come kayaking with me."

I yanked my arm from his grasp. "No, thanks."

Inside I really wanted to say yes and find out more about this mystery boy before me.

"Come on, you'll love it. I promise."

I continued staring at my book, not taking in a word. "I doubt I will. It looks tippy."

I glanced up at him. He blinked. "You've never kayaked? Come on, let me show you how. I have an extra kayak with your name on it."

"Oh, really? What is my name then, Sherlock?"

He laughed. His teeth were so white. They were perfectly straight and damn he was good looking.

"Vikki?"

I shook my head.

"Tina?"

"Nope." I got to my feet and started walking away.

"Elizabeth?"

I continued walking up the hill toward my house.

My brother called out from the back deck, "Lyndsey."

"You jerk! Why would you tell him that?" Was he spying on us?

I turned around and he raised an eyebrow. "Lyndsey. I like that." He grabbed a paddle and held it out in front of him. He won and I lost.

I stomped my feet as we walked over to his kayaks. I put on my life jacket and made my way to the pink kayak he pulled off his dock and up to the sandy beach in front of his cabin.

"Why do you have a pink kayak?"

"It's my mom's, but we use it more than she does. You going to get in or keep yapping?"

"You have thirty minutes, but if I don't like it you will never ask me again."

"Deal."

. . .

12

West Sturgeon was a quiet, smaller lake on the chain of five lakes. Boats did not pass through it as much because they had a hard time fitting under the low bridge and the water was shallow.

I took a couple minutes getting used to holding the paddle in a way that did not strain my arms. But once I got into the rhythm, it felt really good. Almost hypnotizing.

Kevin stayed beside me, watching and helping me as I got into the groove of it.

"Put your phone in the hatch so it doesn't get wet. Use a forward stroke."

I nodded and acted like I knew what he was talking about because he was so good looking, and I did not want to look stupid. I made sure not to let him suspect that I was into him, but when he talked about kayaking, his face lit up and captivated all my attention. His motions were so smooth, radiating charisma I could not stop swooning over.

I stopped paddling to catch my breath, and he stopped, too. "Should we turn back?" he asked.

I wanted to keep going, but my body would not make it. We hadn't even left our lake. "Yeah."

We turned around and headed back to shore. He stopped paddling and I stopped beside him.

He pointed in the water a little ahead of us. "See the loons?"

Two loons turned over upside down and disappeared from our view.

"Where did they go?" I sat up a little taller and searched for them to pop back up.

"Loons are like submarines. They have solid bones so they are less buoyant than most birds. They can dive a lot better. You have to see them underwater. They swim so fast."

From Kevin's words, I began looking at nature in a whole

new way. The loons were here this whole time, and I never knew how amazing they really were.

He looked at everything differently than I did. I was so caught up with my phone and friends, I did not stop to take in what was in front of me. I always felt so secluded at the lake, being so far from town and my friends. Now I was glad because I had Kevin to myself.

Back on shore, Kevin took off his shirt and threw it into the grass before lifting the kayak over his head and carrying it to a spot in the grass. His muscles were stacked and well defined on his thin body. His back was chiseled in the shape of a v. He was smart and sexy and probably a lot of trouble.

He turned around to get the other kayak, and I looked away as I walked through the water and toward my house.

"Where are you going?"

*To take a cold shower.* "To get something to eat."

"You should probably invite me over since I did take you out kayaking, and you did end up loving it. Did you not?"

I shook my head and turned around to keep walking away from him. He caught up to me fast and walked beside me.

"I didn't know you'd be using it against me, so I'd feed you. Isn't there a soup kitchen around here somewhere?"

He laughed and stepped in front of me. His face was so close to mine. "Please? Pretty please?" He stared at my lips as if he might kiss them, and my knees wobbled in response.

"I guess I have no choice if I want to go kayaking again, huh?"

His smile got bigger; his teeth so white they were glowing when he said, "That's the spirit."

I pushed him out of my way.

He rubbed his shoulder where I pushed him. "Well, that

wasn't very nice. I think you need food more than I do. You're a bit hangry," he said flashing me another one of his sexy grins.

I was in trouble.

*Now*

I changed out of my work clothes and into my sweats, a blanket draped around my shoulders. the spring night was brisk, and I was home just in time to watch the sun go down. The sky had a pink glow to it. I loved the lake, and there was no place I'd rather be. I heard my screen door open behind me.

"Hey, girl, what you doing?"

"Maddy! I was hoping you would make it. Did David finally fall asleep?"

Maddy and my brother went through a rough patch after my niece Ariel passed away two years ago, but now they were married for the second time and happier than ever. The thought of losing a child made my chest hurt. She was my niece. I was devastated to lose her at the age of five. They now had David, their baby boy. He would never replace our Ariel, but he was loved just as much.

"Yes. Brad told me I needed a break and to get out of the house and come see you. I'm so glad I get the whole summer to be home with David before I go back to work, but it's nice to have an adult conversation."

I placed my hand on hers. "Ah, the benefits of being a

school librarian with summers off after maternity leave. You are an amazing mom. Now let me get you a glass of red wine."

"See, this is why we're best friends."

I came back with a glass of wine in each hand, having no choice but to top off mine while I poured her a glass.

"Guess who I saw today that I haven't seen in forever?"

She swooshed the wine glass, inhaled deeply, and looked back at me before taking a drink. "Who?"

"Kevin Finney."

I said it just as she took a sip of her wine and she choked on it and coughed. "What? Oh my, how many years has it been now? Is he hot?"

I shook my head. "He looks the same, but different. Older in a good way."

"What did he say? What did you say?"

"I got a call from the drug task force to remove some children from a meth house, and when I arrived at the house he was one of the deputies in the front yard watching the children. He really didn't say much."

She sat on the edge of her chair, clearly hoping for more details. "I'm going to pretend you didn't just catch me off guard with the sadness of having to remove children from a drug home, and instead focus on you." She shook her head. "So, did he recognize you? What am I saying? He recognized you, right?"

I laughed at her enthusiasm. "I'm pretty sure he recognized me. And he's aged well. He was actually a bit ... cold."

"Cold?"

I thought she was going to spit the wine right out of her mouth. "Yeah. It was awkward, and he still hates me."

"That's on him, not you. Although, I'm sure he doesn't

hate you, he was probably just in the whole grumpy cop role. Deputies are so hot. Was he in good shape?"

"They are in good shape, and usually really nice. Kevin was the exception. I guess he has his reasons."

I had no doubt he hated me and despised having to work with me today. Maddy only knew a bit about what happened between us. He was my best friend and it all fell apart.

"I think you should ask him to dinner. His parents still live next door, right?"

I stared over the lake in front of us. The ice had melted off the lake, but the end of May brought in a cold wind. May brought us the hope of summer soon to come. Boating, picnics, days in the sun, sitting on the chairs out at the end of my dock, reading a good book. Those were my summer dreams.

Kevin's face popped into my mind, and I smiled at the memories of his handsome face. I missed the old Kevin so much. The one who was confident and kind.

"They never lived next door. The house was always just their summer cabin, but I don't remember the last time I saw them there."

"It's more like a giant house than a cabin."

I looked in the direction of their huge house. They still had cleaners coming in and out. If they stayed at the house at all, they never came out back by the lake where I could see them. Pine and maple trees separated our places enough that I could not see their house. Their high fence also got in the way.

Maddy snapped her fingers. "Earth to Lyndsey. What are you thinking about?"

"Just the old days. I wish you could have been around when we were younger."

"I'm not sure I would have fallen in love with Brad if I saw how much he tortured you as a child."

I laughed. "That's true, he was pretty terrible although I

know somewhere in his big brother head, he thought he was just doing what big brothers do."

Maddy faced the lake with her eyes shut. The cool wind blew her hair.

The peaceful sound of the waves beating against the shore numbed my aching heart.

We watched the sun set in silence, not a word needed to be said between us. This understood silence was a bond only sisters had. She was not my sister by blood, but more importantly my sister by fate and by choice.

"Speaking of Brad, how is he?"

"This school year has been much better than last year. He's a good principal and now that the Lisa fiasco is finally over, and she got hired on as a teacher somewhere in the Cities, we can finally breathe again."

Lisa had a big crush on my brother, and she made up lies to get him to feel bad for her and somehow make him fall in love with her. Brad finally called her out on the last day of school, and she quit on the spot. Everyone was happy, including the children.

"I can't imagine. After everything she put the two of you through."

Maddy let out a loud exhale. "I've learned a lot about forgiveness these past two years."

"Have you heard anything from Tim?" Hot young rock-climbing instructor, Tim had a mad crush on Maddy. They worked together at the school, but he was no longer there, which was probably a good thing. He was a good distraction for Maddy after Ariel passed away and she and Brad divorced, but I was relieved when Brad and Maddy got together and Tim no longer worked at the school.

"He's teaching at the high school in Hibbing now. He and Brad seem to be getting along pretty well. He was thinking about moving out to the lake. He's just waiting to find a place."

"It's not awkward at all between the two of you?" I could not imagine Brad and Tim being friends after everything that happened. But Tim was very likable, and as long as they were okay with it, I was glad to have him around.

"Lyndsey, are you interested in Tim or something?"

I shook my head. "No, no, no. Not a chance. Did I really give off that vibe?"

She stood up. "Nah, I'm just messing with you. I do want to find Tim a good girlfriend. Let me know if you're ever interested. You know ... if this whole thing with Kevin doesn't work out."

I took the blanket off my shoulders and threw it at her. She laughed, her eyes sparkling off the motion light on my deck. "What? You love me for my bluntness."

"See you tomorrow."

She threw the blanket back to me and I caught it, then waved.


I settled in bed with a book in my hand. I had reread the same line probably fifty times now, and I still could not remember what the paragraph was about. I could not get Kevin off my mind for the life of me.

The temp was close to seventy degrees as I pulled my car up to a trailer home in the middle of nowhere. The trailer park was probably the nicest one in the area, but it had some pretty shady places. The double wide light blue home had a pot of flowers and a newly built wooden deck out front. I knocked at the door and a lovely twelve-year-old girl answered.

"Can I help you?"

"Hi, my name is Lyndsey and I'm a social worker. I was wondering if your mom was around."

She rolled her eyes, her blonde curly hair poofed out. "Mom, it's for you."

"What did I tell you about answering the door? You need to vacuum the living room again, I can't see the lines, and Tyler, what the hell are you doing watching television? Go clean your goddamn room."

The door opened quickly, her red hair curly like her daughter's. "Who the hell are you?"

Her dark eye liner was smeared under her eyes making the green in her eyes pop out. I had a hard time looking away.

"You must be Molly. Hello, I'm Lyndsey Jones, a social worker with the county. Can I come in?"

She pushed the screen door open and turned away. "Why the hell not? Everyone else does."

She made her way into the kitchen and poured a vodka tonic.

"Are you with the goddamn county again? I'm not sure why the hell you're wasting your time over here when you should be across the street at the Hansen's house. Those little shits are always stealing shit and causing hell." She held up the glass so I could reach it. "Vodka tonic?"

"No, thanks, I'm driving." Was this really happening? I'd been a social worker for quite a while now and this was definitely a first. No one had ever offered me a drink on the job before.

"I'm packing to take the kids to Johnny's farm. It's the farm from that movie ... what's that movie called, Tam!" She screamed right into my ear.

Tammy peeked around the corner, vacuum in hand. "What movie?"

"What movie?" She rolled her eyes. "The goddamn movie from that barn we are going to, you idiot." She leaned toward me. "Teenagers are a bitch, am I right?"

I was normally not at a loss for words, but I had no idea how to reply.

"I think you're talking about Iron Will," Tammy said.

Molly jumped around me and in front of her daughter. "You better be on your best behavior, okay? My new man is a keeper, and I don't want you to get in the middle again. You and that friend of yours. She's coming, isn't she?"

"Yes, mom. Jill is coming."

Tammy left the room looking a bit defeated, and Molly stripped off her shirt and threw it on the couch without warning.

Okay, I was a professional, but I felt like her actions were so shocking I could no longer speak. She pulled down her pants and stood there in her bra and underwear. I turned my back to her, respecting her privacy even though she was obviously comfortable in her own skin.

"I'm pretty sure her friend has a little crush on my Johnny. Kids, am I right? She's a homely looking girl with stringy hair and always scared of her own shadow. I let her come with us and play mom since her mother is too busy for her. So sad, right?"

She put on clothes and fluffed her hair in the mirror while she kept talking. "So, who reported on me today? That is why you're here, am I right? Someone was jealous of me and put in a silly report to child protection? I've had you people here way too many times. I'm so sorry they're wasting your time. Now that you see I'm not a crazy bitch beating her children you probably want to head to someone else's house, right? Go find some mothers who are actually abusing their children?"

She gulped down her drink without a single breath.

"You have a son, too?"

"Yeah, he's down the block playing with his friend. I can hardly get him to do anything. The boy is spoiled."

"Does anyone else live here other than you and your two kids?"

"Nope, it's just us. I have an actual job so I'm pretty busy, unlike you. My boyfriend stays over every now and then, like when he wants to get some. Men, am I right?"

I had to focus on my breathing and make sure my lungs were working. She was all over the place, and I was having a hard time keeping up.

"We received a report that you were smoking meth in the home. Do you happen to smoke meth?"

She lit up a cigarette and blew the smoke right in my face. "Are you serious? Do I look like I smoke meth? Not with this skin. Get the hell out of my house."

She poured herself another drink. "And make sure to close the goddamn door on your way out." She turned her back on me and stomped her way down the hall. "Tammy! Tammy, where are you? This living room still looks like shit. Vacuum again, in straighter lines this time."

I walked out the door and closed it behind me. I was blown away by everything that just happened. I had clients who screamed at me, threatened me, called me names, and slammed the door in my face, but I never had someone change right in front of me and start drinking as if child protection was not there. I was not sure what to think at all except that this woman was not okay, and I needed to find a way to help her and her children.

A tidy house, children who were old enough to be home alone and in the home while the mother was drinking. I did not have a case to report, even if her behavior was nowhere near normal. She swore and she wasn't modest, but none of it was enough for a screen in for a new case. The good news was she talked to me and opened up. I was beginning to gain her trust, I think. She obviously was not nervous around me, she just had a temper and was impulsive.

She did not recognize that her behavior would be considered concerning or she just did not care. Her normal was different than my normal. Everyone's normal looked different, and I was not there to judge. I was there to make sure the children were safe and that was what I was going to do. All judgment aside, I was there to help.

I saw the kids and although I did not have a chance to interview them today, I would visit the school and interview them tomorrow when their mother was not around. Hopefully, their mother did not tell them they could not talk to me. That always made my assessments difficult. I needed to somehow get the mother to do a UA for me, but that seemed an impossible task.

# Then

Peanut butter and jelly sandwiches was what I ended up making for my hungry new friend. Kevin was more than appreciative.

"Is this homemade jelly?" he said. "Are these made from actual strawberries from like a farm?"

The answer was yes. My mother was Suzie Homemaker. She loved to cook and can and pick berries. We had beautiful gardens in our yard, including a variety of fruits and vegetables. She had a green thumb and worshipped the sun.

"It's homemade jelly, but my mom has a strawberry garden out back, not a farm."

The June day was hot. We played some volleyball in the water, and I took him jet skiing. He hooted and hollered behind me as I jumped waves created by big boats, and we flew through the air. It was the best day I had in what felt like forever. He reminded me how much I loved the lake, and I could be myself around him.

That night we lay on my trampoline and stared at the stars in the sky.

"When my parents said they wanted to get a summer place

at the lake, I couldn't have been more thrilled. To be living amongst nature and swimming every day was a dream. I had no idea what a Side Lake summer would be like. It's better than I imagined," Kevin said.

"It's different when you live way out here. When I ride the bus to school it takes an hour. It's also hard when my friends are busy, and I'm just hanging out by myself."

"An hour?" He turned onto his side and rested his head on his open hand.

"I begged my parents to get a place in town so I could be closer to school and stores. There is so much more to do in town. The lake life gets lonely sometimes."

"I live in town and sometimes it can feel a bit lonely even when you're surrounded by friends. You'll have your license soon and you can go into town whenever you want. Most people would die to wake up to a beautiful lake right outside their window. I don't think I could ever get bored of this place."

"You wouldn't say that if you lived here in the winter."

He laughed. "I guess that's true, but even in the winter you can do so much outdoors. What about snowmobiling and cross country skiing? Oh, and ice fishing. Man, I'm so jealous. I think you'd be surprisingly disappointed if you ever left the lake. Plus, you're a fun person to be around. I bet you have a lot of friends out here."

"Just my best friend. She lives down the road so we're usually inseparable. She hasn't been around this summer because her mom made her spend the summer in the cities with her aunt as a punishment for her bad grades."

Kevin moved a piece of hair out of my face and stared into my eyes. We stayed like that for what felt like forever. He was the first to break the silence. "What's her name?"

"My friend?"

He nodded. Of course, my friend.

"Kat, short for Katrina."

"I hope I get the chance to meet her."

The moonlight brightened his face and made it hard for me to turn my gaze away. I tried not to stare, but he was so beautiful.

"We're going to have a hell of a summer, and you want to know what?" Kevin said.

I put my hands behind my head, hoping he was going to kiss me. "No, what?"

"First, we'll get your brother back for all the teasing he does to you. How old is he anyway?"

"Eighteen," I said. "He just graduated from high school this year."

"Wow, I thought he was so much older. Not that he acts mature, it's just that he looks older."

"He's got charisma. All my friends have a crush on him. No one believes how much he torments me. They think I'm lucky to have such a popular big brother."

"That must be hard."

He put his hand on mine, sending a jolt through my body and leaving my skin with goosebumps. He pulled away before I could take a breath.

"I'll always be team Lyndsey," he said with a friendly tap on my hand.

I knew at that moment I was head over heels for him. My biggest question was whether or not he felt the same way.

We walked down to the tennis courts at the Side Lake Recreation Center the next day. Kevin was a well-rounded athlete, although he had never played tennis. He was a natural. I'd been playing since I was six years old, but I was tripping over my own feet trying to hit the ball back to him. Even his backhand was flawless.

He whooped me.

We went hiking in the woods after we finished the game, and then walked down to the Side Lake Store for ice cream. He chose superman and I got bubble gum ice cream.

"Look at that boat," he said as we sat on a table in front of the store. I turned my head, but before I caught on there wasn't any boat, he bit the top off my cone and started to laugh.

"Jerk!" I leaned over to bite the top of his ice cream, but he moved too fast.

He laughed and stood up. "Not a chance."

I chased him around the parking lot until I finally caught him, but I was so out of breath, I just panted with one hand on my knee and the other one holding what was left of my cone.

"Sounds like you need to start running more."

I shook my head. "Oh, no. I hate running." I really did hate running. It hurt and sweat was gross. I never understood why people thought running was fun. I hated sweating when I played tennis, but it came with the territory, and I learned to tolerate it. Besides, tennis was fun.

"What do you like to do then? You never kayaked, and you don't run."

I put my head down, afraid to admit the truth. "I waterski, downhill ski, drive water toys and I ... play tennis."

His eyes got wide and his mouth fell open. "Oh. I didn't realize."

"I actually thought I was good. Well, until today."

I pushed him. He lost his balance, and nearly lost his cone.

"Hey!"

I walked in front of him, pretending to be angry.

"I'm sorry. I guess I didn't realize how much I'd end up liking tennis."

I shrugged my shoulders. "The truth is, I'm not really an athlete. I've had to work really hard to do well at tennis."

"I hardly believe that."

"No, seriously. I tried track, even though I hate running, and I tripped over a hurdle and had nine stitches in my nose after landing on the pavement. I tried volleyball, but I broke my nose when my nemesis spiked the ball in my face. I tried basketball but tripped over my own damn feet and sprained my ankle."

"But your passion is obviously in the water. I can't wait to watch you ski. I have wake boarded a couple times, but I'm not very good."

"I highly doubt that. You seem to be good at everything."

"Be ready for disappointment. What else do you like to do?"

"I've never told anyone this before, but I really like to shoot. Sometimes I go with my dad to the range and I'm a pretty good shot."

"Really?" He seemed impressed. "I'm on the trap team myself."

Of course, he was. He'd probably beat me at that, too.

"I'd love to go shooting with you," he said.

"Sounds like a challenge."

He raised an eyebrow. "Yes, it does."


We talked my dad into taking us to the range the next day. Kevin shot first. His rounds all made it on the target with great grouping. I took my stance at the firing line, took a deep breath, and exhaled slowly before I put my finger on the trigger and shot off all my rounds in a much tighter grouping in the center of the bullseye.

Although our headgear muffled the sound, I glanced at him to see his mouth hanging open. I was finally better at something than Kevin, and I couldn't help but smirk. But I could not tell if he was impressed or if I'd hurt his manhood.

For the next hour, I continued to outshoot him. He'd just shake his head, obviously shocked by my mad skills. He was good, but I was better.

My dad glanced at Kevin in the rearview mirror on the way back to the lake. "I bet you didn't expect this one to outshoot you, did you?" He pointed his thumb in my direction.

"No, sir, I didn't. I was pleasantly surprised."

I shook my head, embarrassed to be called out. "Dad, it wasn't a competition." Oh, it totally was, and I was so glad I finally beat him at something.

Kevin rubbed his chin "Where did you learn to shoot like that?"

My dad laughed and glanced at me with a proud smile. "That's what happens when your dad is a police officer. I used to drag her to the range with me all the time. We bonded at the range, right kid?"

"I didn't know you were a police officer," Kevin said. "I'm planning on going into the law enforcement program after I graduate."

"That's great, son. It's the best program in the state. I highly recommend it. I've worked with a lot of fine young police officers who graduated from that program."

Kevin turned to me. "Have you thought about going into the program? Your skills are highly impressive."

My dad answered for me. "She's a natural when it comes to shooting, but I don't think she's really cut out to be a cop. I wouldn't want that life for her, and I don't think she's disciplined enough. Am I right, Lyndsey?"

I nodded. He was right, but hearing him say it hurt.

"I think she'd be a great cop," Kevin said, winking at me.

I felt my face grow hot. "I don't know. It's not exactly an easy world for a woman in a man's field."

"If anyone can do it, it's you." Kevin leaned forward. "So, where are you a cop, sir? Are you a city cop?"

"I'm an officer in Hibbing."

"Do you like it?"

My father rolled down his window halfway. "Do you really want to know?"

"Yes, sir."

"It's not an easy job and sometimes you feel a bit disconnected from the community after dealing with hostile criminals all day. Then I remember I'm a part of a much larger picture of officers trying to clean up the community and help make it safe. It's part of who I am. I'm proud of what I represent, even if we don't get a lot of good recognition from the community all the time."

Kevin nodded and turned away. I could tell he was thinking about what my dad said. Policing was not an easy job, but a part of me ached to become an officer. I dreamed of cleaning up the streets and keeping drugs away from children. Maybe I wanted to be like my father.


The next morning, Kevin was waiting for me at the end of my dock. His feet were in the water, and he was staring over the lake. I took a seat next to him. "What are you thinking about?"


He rubbed his face with both hands. "How much you impressed me yesterday with your shooting skills, and how if you don't become a police officer, it would be a waste of your talent."

I held back my laugh, and it came out a snort.

He laughed and pushed my shoulder gently. "Did you just snort?"

"No."

"Yes, you did. You totally just snorted."

I covered my mouth with my hand.

He tucked a stray hair behind my ear, sending a chill down the back of my spine. He looked so deeply into my eyes, it made me nervous.

"What's so funny?"

"It's definitely not talent. I put in a lot of hours at the range to get that accurate."

"That makes sense."

I laughed again.

"What's so funny now?"

"I was thinking that I never thought I'd be better than you at something."

He put his head down. "You've been surprising me since the day I met you. Watching you shoot ... well, it was hot. I don't know another way to describe it. I never expected that, and I was impressed as hell."

I shied away, unsure of how to reply without sounding arrogant. Complements were hard for me to take in. I never thought about it that way. Shooting was just shooting. Wait, did he just call me hot? The act of being hot? It didn't matter. My feelings for him were expanding out of my control.

He put his hand on top of mine, and I froze, unsure of what to make of it. Before I had a chance to react, he dove into the water and turned to splash me.

I screamed and jumped in. I swam after him as he made his way to the water trampoline in front of his cabin. He was fast.

I sat on the edge and watched him jump higher and higher until he did a back summersault, landing on his feet. The trampoline did not have the spring of a normal trampoline, but that did not stop him. He jumped again, getting a bounce off his spring, and then dove into the water, sending the cold water splashing back at me.

I jumped on the trampoline and tried to spring up as high as I could. I watched his face as he crawled back onto the trampoline and jumped next to me. He jumped just right and sent me flying into the air. I fell backward, my knees collapsing.

I cried out. "Hey!"

He kept stealing my bounce, smirking each time the spring took my legs out from underneath me. After a few minutes, we were both breathing hard and lying on our backs.

I stared at the sky and closed my eyes against the bright sun. A boat went by, a little too close to the trampoline. We both sat up to watch. The boat pulled a guy on one ski. The hooting and hollering from the onlookers made me smile.

He looked over at me. "What are you thinking?"

"That that looks like fun."

He turned back to stare at the boat as it got farther and farther away.

"I can't wait to go out in your boat."

"Me, too."

"So, what's it like having a father as a police officer?"

I crossed my arms around my stomach. "Well, that came out of nowhere. It can be really difficult at times. I worry about him when he goes to work and so does my mom. Cops are sort of looked down on by the general population. They are the ones who save us and go into dangerous places when we run out, but still we judge. He tries not to bring his job home with him, but it's hard because he deals with a lot of angry people."

"Sounds tough."

"It can be, but he does a good job of turning it off."

"He sounds like a really good dad."

"Sometimes he can be a little military like, and sometimes I feel like I have to work really hard for him to see me. "

"How would he feel if you decided to follow in his footsteps and become a police officer?"

"You heard him in the car. He would probably try to talk me out of it."

He nodded, as if he was trying to understand and then he picked me up and put me over his shoulders like a sack of potatoes. He always did that when our conversations got too serious. He liked to lighten the mood.

I hit his back and wiggled to get out of his grasp. "Put me down! Put me down, Kevin. I'm serious." I was not serious. I loved our playful banter and every second his hands were on me.

"Oh, well, if you're serious." Instead of putting me down, he walked closer to the water and leaned forward.

I yelled out, "No!" But it was too late. We both fell into the water. I smiled.

*Now*

I stopped at the post office in Side Lake to pick up my mail.

Erma looked at me, a mop in hand. "Lyndsey, how are you?"

I smiled back at her. "I'm doing good."

"Did you hear Troy Finney is getting married?"

I held my breath. After all these years, I had not heard anyone speak a word in my small community about the Finneys, and now I was working alongside Kevin and his brother was getting married. As far as I knew, the Finneys had not been at their cabin in years. I was unsure of the last time I saw Kevin's brother, let alone his mother.

"No, who is he marrying?"

She held the mop in front of her small five-foot frame. "A girl who used to camp at Pine Beach with her family. A Victoria something? I think she dated Brad when you guys were younger."

"Victoria?" I only knew one Victoria. "Did she have a brother, Ethan?"

She slid the mop over the floor again before taking another break. "Yeah, Ethan. That's his name."

35

"Wow, good for them. I had no idea they were even together."

Brad was going to be shocked. Would they even invite him to their wedding? Would they invite any of us?

"How's Brad doing? I haven't seen much of him lately. He seems so busy now, with the new baby and all."

Everyone knew everyone and everything in the small town. When Ariel passed away, a heavy black cloud fell over the town. The locals were like one big family who took care of their own. But a small town also had its faults. Hiding secrets was more difficult.

"He's doing really good. David's getting so big."

"Your brother and Madeline are always in my prayers."

I nodded with a small smile and opened my mailbox with my key and took out the bulk of mail. "Thank you."

She nodded and turned back to her mopping.

I waited until I got home before sifting through the pile of mail. Mostly junk mail, as expected, then a pink envelope got my attention. I opened the letter handwritten in calligraphy.

*Join us in celebrating the wedding of Victoria Lynn Iverson and Troy Richard Finney at the Finney's family cabin in Side Lake, Minnesota.*

The invitation made it official. I was invited to Kevin's brother's wedding, along with the majority of Side Lake. If I went, I would see Kevin, and I would be there without a plus one. Would Kevin be there with someone? Did he have any kids? Why did I care so much?

"What are you staring at?"

I jumped to my feet at the sound of Brad's voice, and the invitation flew out of my hand. I picked it up off the floor and hit him with it, punching his shoulders until my heart finally relaxed. "You scared the crap out of me, Brad! I need to start locking my doors, you know that?"

"What you got there?" He snatched the invitation out of my hand and held it above my reach.

I chewed on my nails and studied his face. I never realized how much he looked like my dad until that moment. His nose, his eyes, his strong jawline.

"Troy is getting married? You've got to be kidding me. I better be invited. Do you know this Victoria?"

I shook my head. "Look at the name again, Brad."

"Victoria Iverson?"

"As in one of your girlfriends from back in the day. Ethan's sister."

"Oh, wow, Victoria and Troy, huh? I had no idea they were even together. We were together all the time that one summer. It's been so long since I've talked to either of them."

Once the Finneys let the trees grow in between our cabins, it seemed a giant fence separated us. I'm not even sure they knew Brad bought a house on our road.

"No. I don't think I'm even friends with him on Facebook."

Kevin would not be on Facebook, not with his job. We went by our first and middle names on Facebook, which made it more challenging for clients to hunt us down and analyze our personal lives when they were pissed off. I could not imagine being a police officer and what challenges they had if they wanted social media presence.

"Kevin's a deputy now so I highly doubt he's on Facebook."

"How do you know? Have you seen him?"

I wished Maddy had broken our sister bond just this once,

and told him about my run-in with Kevin the other day, so I did not have to relive it.

"I saw him briefly when I had to remove some kids from a meth house. He was one of the deputies."

He grinned. "I'm so glad I don't have your job. Still the lovers' quarrel, huh?

"There is no lovers' quarrel. We just went in different directions."

He looked at me sideways. "Sure, whatever you say."

"I'm serious."

He shook his head. "Whatever you say. I'm going to see if Maddy picked up the mail. If you got invited, I better have been invited."

He pulled his phone out of his pocket and typed something into it. It dinged almost immediately.

"Maddy said we got an invite. How did they even know we lived here? Small town, I guess. You're going, right?"

Although the last thing I wanted was to see Kevin in my personal life, I did want to go. I had not seen Troy or his parents in almost a decade. As far as I knew we were still on good terms. I just hated being around Kevin. He still gave me butterflies, and I hated that he had that effect on me.

"I'm not sure. I have to see Kevin enough at work now."

"Oh, come on. The two of you were inseparable for years. You need to get over it," Brad said as he messed up my hair. I ducked out of the way.

"Is mom at the nursing home with dad?"

"She pretty much lives there when she's not at Auntie Jess's."

After dad almost died last summer, he ended up in a nursing home. Mom could not take care of him and I worked every day, so he would not get the twenty-four hour care he needed at home. We considered a nurse coming to the house, but with all the insurance issues, it was not a possibility yet.

My mother was on me daily to bring him home, but we all knew he was better off in the nursing home. He had fallen and broken his hip twice now, and my mother was not doing so well herself. She was diagnosed with dementia but somehow, she was still driving. She moved out and stayed with her sister. and I got the house.

I did feel a bit guilty about it. I still liked to stop in and take care of her in town as much as I could, but she only let me come once a week because she wanted me to have a social life. Auntie Jess agreed, and I was doing my best to give her some space, but it was hard.


He poured himself a glass of wine. "Don't you dare feel bad about dad not coming home. You need to stop taking care of everyone else. Start going on some dates, live your life. Auntie Jess and mom are right."

I took the bottle out of his hand and poured myself a glass. "You sound like Maddy."

"Well, she's right, you know. You need to start thinking about yourself for a change. Life goes by way too fast. You deserve to be happy."

"I know, but I worry about them. It's why I'm the favorite," I said with a smirk.

"You wish. Well, I better get back so Maddy can go for her run. Will you be joining her?"

I laughed. "You know I don't run. I can watch the babe if you want to go with her."

He looked away as if he was really considering it. "I would take you up on that, but I think you need some time to yourself. I'm serious, you need to listen to us and start thinking about yourself for a change. It isn't healthy. Every choice you make is for someone else. Who is looking out for you?"

Brad left without waiting for me to answer. I grabbed my

glass of wine and a book and went outside to sit in my cushioned chair. I put my feet up on the footrest and took a deep breath as I gazed at the lake.

In a few weeks we would be putting out the dock and the boat. I closed my eyes to imagine the feeling of the hot sun on my face as we cruised across the lake. I may be living at my parents' house in my early 30s, but this was my dream house, and I would not want it any other way. My brother was wrong, I did not need a man in my life, and I definitely did not need Kevin Finney in my life. He may be easy to look at, but he was as stubborn as they came, and I did not need that.

"Good morning, everyone. We have three new cases this morning. An INV and two-family assessments. Who is up next?"

I raised my hand.

My boss looked at me. "Lyndsey, it looks like you're already open on this one. We received another screen in for Molly Eiler. Looks like her ex made a report that she had been smoking meth in her home with her children present. One of the kids, it looks like the boy, found some white crystals and she hit him with a closed fist when he asked her what they were. The father wasn't sure how many times she hit him and where, but that's for you to investigate. It says here the father was hesitant to give out more information. Sounds like she's threatening him with seeing his kids. Be careful what information you give her on this report. We need his trust so he will keep informing us about what is going on there."

I cleared my throat. "I am always careful in what I say. I'm not surprised she's threatening him. Some shady crap is going on there. Yesterday, she changed her clothes right in front of me like it was no big deal, and she offered me a vodka tonic.

She won't be happy about this report. She's not a big fan of social workers."

Everyone around the table agreed with nods of support or they laughed. Not many people liked social workers. Television and movies portrayed us as angry, demanding women without hearts who get all dressed up in expensive clothes and high heels to rip children from their parents' arms without any reason.

"I could come with you if you'd like me to do a safety plan with her," Mary said.

"I'm not sure we're there yet. I'll see if I can get her to agree to setting one up later in this week or early next week."

This would be a difficult conversation to have with her after yesterday, and I hated that I had to tell her about a new report. She would know where the report came from, and that the father was the only safe person for the children.

"Molly likes me, I'll go," Tracey said.

No way in hell was I bringing Tracey with me. The only thing she was good at was flirting with cops and believing everything a client said and then closing up the case. She would drag me down. The investigation would not be thorough if she was in charge."

"I'm good," I said getting up. "There are two other cases I'm sure you could take."

She scowled at me and exchanged an eye roll with Hannah who, for some reason, worshipped Tracey.

"Great idea, Lyndsey. I think you're up for a case, Tracey, and since you're so excited to tag along, why don't you go out with her, Hannah?"

I walked out the door with a smile plastered across my face. My boss was good at her job. She knew who was working their cases, and who was not. Tracey was evil and angry, and had not changed one bit since college. My job was stressful enough, I did not need her on my case all the time. She was always doing something to get under my skin, and it worked every time.

I grabbed the keys for the van and placed the Eiler file in my bag. I had a half hour drive to prepare for the confrontation that was soon to come.

*Then*

Kat returned from her aunt's house in the Cities in mid-August. I was laying on the sand with Kevin when she walked up.

"Hello," she said, in a high-pitched voice.

I turned around to see my friend, who I no longer recognized. Her hair had highlights, and her see-through cover up hardly covered up the cleavage showing in her risqué swimsuit. I did a double take at the amount of makeup she was wearing for a day at the lake.

Kevin stood up to see who was joining us, and her eyes slowly rolled down his torso and stayed there. In no way discreet. She definitely liked what she saw.

I gave her a hug anyway, and when we pulled away, her eyes returned to Kevin.

Her obvious interest in my guy as if I was not there at all dumbfounded me.

She rested her hands on her hips with a whole lot of attitude. "I'm gone for two months and this hot stud has taken my place?"

He held out his hand and grinned. "Hi, I'm Kevin. And you are?"

"Kat," she said arching her eyebrows. "Meow." Then came the air claw.

I was embarrassed for her. What happened to my somewhat modest friend?

She pulled on her swimsuit to bring his eyes back to her chest.

I slapped my hand to my forehead. My secondhand embarrassment was likely showing on my now red face.

He raised an eyebrow at her in return. "Hello. Kat, meow, is it?" He emphasized the meow.

His sexy dimples had me blushing, and he was not even looking at me.

"You know it." She looked past him and right at me. "Is this what you've been hiding? I'm so pissed off that I wasn't here to stare at those abs all summer." She looked back at him. "Do you live around here?"

He shook his head. "I have a feeling you're trouble."

She laughed and waved him off as if it was a compliment. She had been home five minutes and I was ready for her to leave. This was another side to her I'd never seen before.

I coughed in an attempt to bring their attention back to me. "His parents bought the cabin next door. He's been a real pain in the ass," I said, then sent a smirk in his direction to show Kat he was my guy.

He turned around quickly, his mouth open. "Hey, come on. Who taught you how to kayak and swam with you all summer?" He looked back at Kat. "I even got her to lighten up a little bit."

This got Kat's attention. "Lyndsey? You need to tell me your trick."

I stood up and put my hands on my hips. "Hey, hey. Come on, guys."

They both laughed and Kat put her hand up in the air, Kevin high-fived her.

Jealousy flowed through my veins.

"You said you guys went kayaking? I want to go. I've been in the car for four hours, and I'm in desperate need of some exercise."

"I wish, but I only have two kayaks," Kevin said, pointing out the two that lay bottom up on the shore.

"Well, that stinks," she said.

"You guys go ahead. I have some other things I want to do anyway." I pushed my hair behind my ears, and hoped one of them would say they did not want to go without me.

"Are you sure?" Kevin said.

No such luck.

Kat grabbed my hand. "Yeah, are you sure? I just got here, and I want to spend time with my best friend."

They were not saying no. All the air squeezed out of my lungs, and I could no longer look at either of them. What did I just do? "We can hang out later. You two go ahead." Why did I feel the need to punish myself?

They looked at me and then back at each other.

*Please don't go.*

Kevin shrugged his shoulders and turned back to Kat. "I'll take you for a quick one."

I headed for my deck and watched as they paddled away. They splashed each other and laughed. I wanted to hide in my room and cry, but instead I took a hot shower and then I hid out in my room and cried. They would probably be in love by the time they got back and forget all about me anyway.

. . .

I fell asleep and woke up to Kat jumping on my bed. I pushed her off the bed, and she fell to her knees on the floor with a laugh. "Hey! You could have hurt me."

"And you could have broken my bed jumping on it like that," I said.

"I can't help it. I'm so excited to be back. I really had a good time kayaking. We need to do that more."

"I'm glad you had fun." I hoped she would catch the sarcasm and passive aggressiveness in my voice. I looked away as I said the words so she could see how angry I was, in case she somehow missed it.

"It was so awesome. I'm pretty sure I'm in love."

I turned around and found her hugging my pillow with a huge smile. Was she being serious?

"I had my first kiss, and it was a-mazing."

I jumped to my feet. I'd absolutely had it. It was one thing for her to come in and take time away from me hanging out with the most amazing and gorgeous guy I'd ever known, but for her to steal him from right under me like that. Enough was enough.

Her smile quickly faded when she saw my fisted hands and my cold eyes glaring at her.

"What's wrong? Oh, no. You don't have a crush on Ethan do you?"

Did I hear her right? Was she saying she kissed a guy named Ethan? Not Kevin? Did she maybe think Kevin's name was Ethan?

"You don't even know his name? Really? It's Kevin, not Ethan. You're so clueless, I don't even know who you are anymore."

"No, not Kevin. Ethan. We met him at Sixberry's Landing. We went under the bridge, and he was there, in the water, holding onto a boat."

I held my hand to my heart. "You could have said that in the first place. I thought you kissed Kevin."

She jumped to her feet and held onto my hands.

"I wouldn't do that to you. I kissed a guy named Ethan. Do you know Ethan?"

I finally took a breath. "We were so close to not being friends anymore," I said dropping onto my bed. "I don't know a Ethan."

She jumped onto her knees and hugged me. She did not notice I was not hugging her back. It was too soon.

"I would never let anything get between us, and it's obvious Kevin has a crush on you."

"It is?"

"Oh, yeah. I could cut that sexual tension with a knife. He was a perfect gentlemen."

I could only think about how into Kat he seemed. I thought he flirted with me, but the way he acted with her made me believe I was reading him wrong.

"Yes, it is. All he did was ask about you and tell me how much fun the two of you were having. I'm so happy for you. He's so hot. I mean, he isn't as cute as Ethan, but he's still pretty cute."

"Oh, Kat. I guess I'll have to meet this Ethan."

"His family are permanent campers at Pine Beach. He's here until school starts."

"That's great."

"How about we give each other pedicures and you can tell me all about your summer with Kevin, okay? Then we can talk about Ethan and my summer in the Cities, okay?"

I smiled. Maybe my old friend was in there somewhere.

"How about French manicures?"

"Even better."

*Now*

Molly worked until three o'clock in the afternoon. Her children would come home from school shortly after. I checked on some other clients in the area before I went there. I had thirty open cases and not enough time to be the social worker I wanted to be. Paperwork took up a good chunk of the job, and we had to time record into the system everything we did all day. We literally had to time record the amount of time it took us to time record. How could we be efficient if we were spending most of our time at a desk? When we did our jobs and investigated the cases as deeply as we should, we would mess up on our time recording. Then our hours were cut so instead of a full forty hour week, we worked thirty-seven and a half hours.

We did not have a choice when it came to overtime. Our jobs came with sitting in the emergency room while we waited for a child to get checked out after being physically abused, not being given his medications by his parents, or in the worst cases, waiting for a child to get clearance after they were sexually abused. Those cases were the hardest for me to investigate.

I had cases where children were locked in their bedrooms

with only a bucket to pee in. They never came out of their rooms. I had cases where the children were burned with hot irons, whipped with belts, where parents withheld food, and neglect cases where the parents did not come home at all.

I've been in meth homes with dealers, and my life has been threatened. I had a chair thrown at me once, and my finger was slammed in a door. I have been called every cuss word in the book, and I've even been recorded talking to a client while live on Facebook.

My job has not been easy, and I've been stressed to the point where my gums bled. I have had trouble sleeping some nights because I was so worried about a child being returned to an abusive home when we did not have enough evidence to prove which parent cracked the baby's skull, so the baby was sent home to be with the abusive parents. I was burnt out after three years on the job.

Everyone thinks the social worker is the one who decides whether a child should be taken from their home for permanency, when a parent loses their custody rights, or that a social worker is responsible when a child is put back in a home where their safety is in jeopardy. But that's not accurate. I remove a kid with a police hold when an officer agrees it is in the best interest of the child.

I do everything I can to find a relative who can take in the child or children for a day or two, maybe a week or sometimes it ends up being forever, I never really know. When there is no one, I call foster care licensing social workers within the county, and they help me to find a home for the children. Sometimes a home is not available because there aren't enough foster homes to take in the children. When that happens, I call the local crisis shelter for abused and neglected children, and hope they have enough room to take them in.

After all that is done, I write a pre-petition screening. I meet with a county attorney, explain why the children need to be removed from their home, and why it is unsafe. The county attorney decides if we have enough evidence to appear in front of a judge. I testify in court and wait on the final decision from the judge about removal. Every now and then I get lucky, and the parent signs a voluntary agreement. I then place the children somewhere safe until the parent gets the help they need.

Was it always safe when the child returned to their home? No. It's my job to keep an eye on all these families to make sure a child's life is not in jeopardy. But there isn't enough time in the day to do all we need to do. We investigate calls from reports to determine which ones are enough to meet the statute. False reports have been made because the parents are going through a bad divorce and want to punish the other parent, or win, by making them look bad and report them to CPS. They don't understand the person they hurt the most is the child caught in between their parents' divorce.

The community tends to get angry when we screen calls. They have complained we aren't doing our jobs, or we need to do more. They don't see that we can only do so much within the laws. They don't see how hard we work to sift through everything. They don't understand that a child wearing dirty clothes due to lack of money is not really a huge issue compared to children who are not being fed, or are given drugs or alcohol as rewards.

My job has been hard and stressful, and turnover constantly keeps us shorthanded. We are disrespected, and every day I tell myself I am going to quit. But I haven't quit, and I don't know if I ever will, because I'm good at my job. I am good with children, and I put everything I have into each case, but that leaves me exhausted.

I knocked at Ida's door and little four-year-old, Mya, opened it just a sliver so I could see part of her face.

"Is your grandma here?" I said in my sweetest voice

because she was likely still traumatized by everything that happened yesterday, and I may not be her favorite person.

She kept peeking through the crack. The door was only open wide enough for me to see her eye.

"Mya, let me talk to the social worker, okay? Back up a little bit so I can get the door open."

With her grandmother's words, Mya ran off, her hair flopping around as she hid in what looked to be the kitchen.

Ira's house was clean and hoarder free. Not perfect or spotless, but lived in. There were books on the floor, a blanket in the middle of the living room, a couple pillows on the floor, and toys shoved on a shelf. It looked ... safe. I smiled to myself, relieved at finding a safe home for them.

"Sorry about that. What is your name again?"

"Lyndsey," I said.

I stepped into the house and wiped my feet. I never take off my shoes in case we have to run, or if something hazardous was in the home. "How are you, Ida? How is everything?"

"Have a seat." She pointed to the couch, and she sat in the recliner.

"It's going about as good as expected. The boys seem to be doing okay, but Mya had nightmares last night. I had no idea my daughter was into the drugs again. I just don't understand why she does this."

She looked around and I suspected she was making sure the kids could not hear her.

"I told her the last time I was going to get custody of the kids if she took anymore drugs. I'm too old to be raising my grandchildren, but someone has to help them. I don't get why she does it."

"It sounds like you have been through a lot with everything going on with your daughter."

"I have, but it's the children who matter. I've raised my kids, why can't she do the same?"

She was fidgeting with her hands after wiping a tear.

"They're lucky to have you." I smiled at her, meaning every word. "Not everyone has family who is this supportive. It gives your daughter a huge chance at changing her ways when she has someone as supportive as you are to help her when she decides she's ready to get sober. I'm here to help in any way I can."

"Thank you. I always thought social workers were women on a power trip who got picked on in high school or something. I'm glad you aren't."

She had no idea how much her words meant to me. Sometimes I felt like I was not doing enough.

She wiped a tear and my heart hurt for her.

"So, what's next?" she asked.

"Well, since she signed a voluntary placement agreement, you have temporary custody. I ask that you don't let her see the kids until she can sober up. If she shows up, call the police. I know that's a hard thing to do, but I'm here to help every step of the way."

She nodded. "I understand."

"What do you need for the kids?"

She looked around her living room as if looking for answers. "Well, they need clothes and some more toys." She covered her eyes with her palms. "I'm too old for this."

I shot her a small smile. "You're doing great. Really."

A loud bang and then little feet running down the stairs made us both stop and look. One of the little boys barreled down the stairs in a panic. "Tommy broke my Legos, grandma. He did it on purpose."

Tommy's head hung down as he sat on the stairs.

"Tommy? Did you do that on purpose? You know your brother has been building that ship all day." She stood up and looked at me. "I'm sorry, I'd better take care of this. Is there anything else you need from me?"

I stood. "Why don't you send me the kids' sizes and I will see what I can do about some money for new clothes. I'll let you know as soon as I find anything out."

"Thank you," she said, with absolute sincerity. "Thank you for helping the children."

"I promise you, I will do everything I can to make sure they're safe. I appreciate all you are doing and please don't hesitate to give me a call if you need anything."

*Then*

Kat and I spent the next hour talking about my summer with Kevin. She was becoming a little jealous about not being around, so I changed the subject to focus on her.

"Tell me about your summer at your aunt's house. What was it like?"

She filed my nails, her hands slowing down as if she was deep in thought. She looked up at me. "It was okay. My aunt lives on a farm in a rich area, so it wasn't horrible. I did meet some guys while I was playing tennis at the community center there. An upscale version of our rec center, but the hot guys there, you would not believe." She squeezed the nail file in her fists with excitement.

"You seem like a different person from the person you were when you left."

"I feel different. I loved not having to be around my mom. She's so uptight and always watches over my shoulder and tells me what to do and what not to do. My aunt may be my mom's sister, but she is nothing like her. She's easy going, and she even let me go to the mall and hang out with guys I met at the community center. Can you believe that?"

"That's great. I'm glad it wasn't all bad."

"I can't believe my mom sent me away. I hate her."

Hate was a strong word. Sure, her mother was a bit over the top, but I doubted she actually hated her. My mother was a bit over the top at times, too, but she would never send me away.

"I worked on my aunt's farm and she even paid me. Oh, man, those farmers out there are so hot. I had a lot of fun, but I missed my summer in Side Lake with you. Nothing compares to a Side Lake summer."

"I can't believe you got to hang out with boys. Did you mess around with them? Lose your v card?"

She laughed. "Kiss, yes. But I kept my v card. Come on, we were in public most of the time. I think I'd use it with Ethan though, if the opportunity arises."

They just met. No way was she serious.

"I'm serious," she said, reading my thoughts. "I missed a whole summer at the lake. I need to make up for lost time. Although I had fun, we wait all year for the weather to get warm enough to spend it swimming and boating, or laying on McCarthy's Beach, scoping out the guys."

"We do appreciate our summers after the brutal Minnesota winters."

"So true. When I graduate I'm moving somewhere warm."

I put my hand on top of hers and stopped her from filing my pinky nail down to nothing. The heat from the friction was burning my nail.

I put my hand on top of the file to stop her. "I think my nail is filed the best it's going to get."

She laughed. "I'm sorry, I guess I was a bit distracted."

"So, tell me about this Ethan. You guys weren't kayaking very long. Tell me details."

"Yes, Ethan. Oh, he's so hot." Her whole demeanor changed. The sparkle was back in her eyes. "Okay, so we were kayaking across the lake and went under the bridge and when we came out by Sixberry's Landing, Ethan was there standing in the water, holding a boat by a rope, like I said. Kevin asked if he needed any help since he was all alone. His dad had a flat tire on his trailer and had to run and get his spare. Ethan was holding the boat until he came back."

No wonder I had no idea who this Ethan was, he was just at the landing to take his boat out of the water after what I guessed was a day boating on the chain. "So he doesn't live around here?"

"He and his family are permanent campers at Pine Beach. Did I forget to mention that? Anyway, he was pulling his boat out of the water to take it to the gas station. It must have been low on gas or something. I don't know, I was a little preoccupied to ask too many questions."

"But where is he from? Is this his first year staying at the campground?"

"I guess he lives up north somewhere, and I believe it's his first year at the lake, but he never really said. I was too busy nibbling on his lips. They were really nice lips."

"Kat!"

She smirked innocently at me. "What?"

"How did you even make out with him that fast? Where was Kevin when this was taking place?"

I put away all the nail polish as she kept talking.

"I'm getting there. Just listen, okay?"

"Oh, I'm listening."

"So, anyway, he was left there until his dad or whatever came back, it's not important. He looked bored, so Kevin and I put our kayaks on shore and sat with him and took turns holding the boat so he could get a break."

"How unselfish of you," I said, a teasing tone in my voice.

She rolled her eyes. "Anyway, one thing led to another, and Kevin went into the woods to pee, and Ethan and I kissed."

I grabbed onto her arm. "What? Like that fast? How long did Kevin pee?"

She shrugged. "Just a minute or two."

"Wow. Did you guys exchange numbers or anything?"

She stood up, her hands on her hips. "Of course, we did. This guy is hot, Lyndsey. Like hot hot. Not just like average hot."

Her attitude was nothing new. My best friend was boy crazy. She was no longer shy in that department. I envied how confident and flirty she was around guys now. I tended to get a little shy and lacked confidence where she stood out.

"What else happened?"

She let out an annoyed grunt. "Kevin cock blocked me."

I burst out laughing. "He what?"

"They started talking about hunting and boating and ... I think your friend is clueless. He seriously stole him right from under my nose."

"Kevin is pretty friendly and outgoing. He was the same way toward me when we first met this summer."

"Yeah, well Ethan gave Kevin his number so they could go fishing or something dumb, and I put it in my phone."

Maybe she was not as good with guys as I thought. "So, let me get this right. He didn't give you his number, you just put it in your phone when he told Kevin his number?"

"Well, when you put it like that ... I mean, I think he said it so I would hear it."

"I'm not saying it isn't a possibility."

She picked up a pillow on my bed and hit me with it. I grabbed it from her grasp and hit her back. She grabbed another pillow and hit me again, but a little harder this time.

She laughed. "You're screwing up my nail polish."

By the time we stopped the pillow fight, our hair was messy, our nails ruined from grasping the pillows so tightly, and we were both out of breath. Our faces were flushed.

My brother forced the door open without knocking. "Kevin is here with some guy. They are downstairs waiting for you dorks."

Kat's eyes were on me. She squealed. "You know you can't have boys in your room unless your door is open," Brad said. He pushed my door and held it so it did not swing back before he disappeared.

I turned to Kat. "Want to go to the docks?"

"Sounds good to me."


Ethan sat at the end of the dock and put his bare feet in the water. Kat sat down beside him, playfully kicking his feet with hers.

Ethan was handsome in that blonde high school quarterback kind of way, with broad shoulders. I could see why she was so into him as I watched her flip her hair behind her shoulder and let out a squeaky laugh. A bit overdramatic for my taste. She had gone from my outgoing, yet conservative best friend, to this boy crazy flirt after returning from the Cities.

Out of nowhere they started kissing. Kevin and I exchange glances in surprise and shock.

I wanted to get away from the awkward moment. "Would you like to go for a walk?" I said to Kevin.

He did not hesitate. "Sure."

"We're heading over to Kevin's. Catch up with you guys later," I said as we left. We kept walking, and there was no response from them. They were too busy shoving their tongues down each other's throats.

At Kevin's house, we climbed the stairs to his beautiful wrap around porch, overlooking the lake. A hot tub sat in the center of the porch. He unlocked the cover.

"You know I don't have a swimsuit, right?"

His eyes glazed with need, challenging me. "I figured."

Together, we folded the cover over, and it slipped down the side of the hot tub. His hungry eyes peered through the darkness at me.

No way was I stripping my clothes off right there.

In one swift motion, he jumped up and sat on the edge of the tub, bypassing the stairs.

I took the safe way, and used the stairs. I sat down a good foot away from him.

"You aren't going commando, are you?"

"Kevin. Really?"

Was he hitting on me? Was this for real?

"Your bra and underwear are pretty much the same as a swimsuit, you know. Unless you're too modest."

He was challenging me. His dark eyes sparkled in the light.

Kevin was nowhere near as ripped or tall as Ethan. He was toned but thin, and handsome and confident and ... I needed to stop thinking about him. He was my friend, nothing more. Yet here he was telling me to take off my clothes and get in the hot tub in my bra and underwear. Giving off vibes that best friends did not exactly give to each other.

"This is weird. I'm not taking off my clothes, but you go ahead." I wanted to, I really wanted to but I was scared to risk our friendship. I did not want to be just another girl to him, even if his words made me warm all over.

He shrugged and confidently took off his clothes, his eyes staring at me. Every muscle in my body burned with desire. Off came his clothes, and I turned away to hide the heat in my cheeks.

When I turned back, he was under the water and the jets were turned on. I took my sandals off and put my feet in the water.

I could not stand the silence. I had to say something. "So, you never told me where you actually live."

He sat up a little straighter in the hot tub and rested his arm on the side. I had a hard time not imagining what it would be like to snuggle into his chest, while his arm wrapped around my shoulders, pulling me in close.

"I could have sworn I told you I was from Duluth."

I shook my head. "Nope, I think that is something I would remember. Do you like living there? I love Duluth. There's so much more to do there." I was rambling. Shut up, Lyndsey.

He ran his hands through his wet hair, taunting me. Challenging me to try to stay away. Damn him

"It's alright. It has its problems like any other place. Sure, we have more to do, but there are also more people. Don't make me start on the hills. Try driving down them in the winter when it's slick and you can't stop. And how often we have to change our breaks. With so many people and tourists, it's nothing like Side Lake in the summer."

Now he was rambling.

"It's so beautiful in Duluth though, and the lake effect makes it warmer in the winter, right?" I knew the answer, but I wanted to hear him talk. I loved to hear the passion in his words and the animation as he talked with his hands as much as with his words.

"Yeah, but the wind is awful. I mean, it's beautiful, but I'd love to live here. You're in the middle of the woods surrounded by stars and water. I can't get enough."

"Really? I love the lake, but I always imagined myself moving to a bigger city. Maybe Minneapolis or New York."

He moved closer to me, just inches from my legs hanging into the warm water. He bumped my leg, and a chill ran up my spine even though I was sweating from the rising steam.

"You don't come off as a big city girl to me."

What was that supposed to mean? "Why do you say that? What kind of girl do I come off as?"

He moved closer and rested his chin on my knees. If I

wasn't so offended by his judgment, it would have affected me more. My legs tightened up at his touch.

"Oh, lighten up. I didn't mean anything bad. I just think of you as this sweet, nature-loving sharpshooter."

"That's really funny. The truth is I love all of those things, but I want to get away. I want to see what big city life is all about."

The bubbles turned off and Kevin dunked his head under the water. He came up and shook his head like a wet dog. I held out my hand in defense, but it was too late. I was already soaked.

I looked down at my shirt.

"Oops, did I get you wet?"

"You jerk." I swiveled my feet out of the water.

He reached out to help me, but instead of helping me, he caught me off balance and pulled me into the hot tub and onto his lap.

"I can't believe you did that!"

I splashed him, and he put his arm around my neck and pulled me close to his chest. I quit fighting with him, and his grip loosened. I stood up in the hot tub and saw his mouth hanging open as he held my gaze. I glanced down and knew he could see what I was seeing. My clothes were tightly pulled against my body, leaving little to the imagination. I crossed my arms in front of my chest and turned away to climb out.

He grabbed my hand again and pulled me into the water. I felt the electricity between us. He turned me around and held me close. Our faces were inches away from each other. His warm breath was on my face. Was he going to kiss me?

A loud noise broke our connection.

"Kevin, get out of that hot tub now. Lyndsey, is that you? You really shouldn't be in there in your clothes. The tub has chlorine, you know. It'll ruin your clothes."

I smiled at Kevin, and then looked back at his mother.

"Sorry, Mrs. Finney. It definitely wasn't planned. Kevin here thought it would be funny to pull me into the water."

"I don't know what she's talking about," he said, but he held onto my arm under the water so I could not move or get out.

His mother frowned. "Kevin, you don't push people into a hot tub ever. Come on. I think you're old enough to know better."

He let go of my hand. I climbed out and walked away from him. I turned back when his mother was far enough way. "Yeah, Kevin."

He raised his eyebrows at me, smiled, and said, "Fine, you go home and change, but after your shower, you're coming back for a bonfire."

I turned away without a word, but we both knew I'd be back.

*Now*

I pulled up in front of the familiar trailer. A sheriff's car was parked a couple houses down. Of course, Finney was the investigator on this case. I would be working with him again. How did I avoid him for all those years and now I'm suddenly working two investigations with him?

I pulled up right out front. Molly's bright red Eclipse was parked nearby.

Kevin got out of his car and turned down the radio volume on his shoulder as he moved closer. He nodded in the direction of her car.

"Well, it looks like we caught her home, huh?"

I forced a smile. "Yep."

"How does she afford this nice vehicle?" He stopped to examine it. "There isn't a bit of rust on it. Looks like she just had it waxed even."

"She's in the plumber's union. She can definitely afford it." I walked up the steps, then leaned back. "Expect the unexpected with this one. She always surprises me. I have never seen someone make so much money and be so broke all the time."

He laughed. "It doesn't matter how much money she makes if she spends it faster than she makes it. At least she has a good job. It's hard to surprise me these days. I feel like I've seen it all."

I smiled because there was no way he had never met anyone like Molly. She was one-of-a-kind. I knocked on the door. A shadow moved inside.

"Who the hell is it?" Molly said in her deep voice. She threw open the door and when she saw me, her eyes turned cold.

"Why the hell are you bothering me again? And why the hell did you bring a cop with you? I did nothing wrong. "

"We've received a new report, Molly. Can we come in?"

"Do I have a choice?"

She threw up her hands, and walked over to her counter where her bottle of whisky was standing and poured some into a lowball glass.

"If you're driving your children anywhere today, you shouldn't be drinking," Kevin said.

His tone came out a little copish, but could I blame him? She was pulling out straight whisky at one o'clock in the afternoon.

She lifted the glass with a challenging glance. "I'm not. They ride the bus." She raised the glass in toast-like fashion, tipped her head back, and took the whole shot.

We stood there in silence as she shook her head and grunted in reaction to the shot.

"Can you chat with us for a minute? I'd like you to be sober when we talk about this with you," I said.

"Let me guess, you have more paperwork for me to sign."

I forced a friendly smile. "Nope. Not today. We're actually here about a new report that there may possibly be some meth in the home? Also, allegations that you hit your son. Remember, these are just allegations so we are here to talk with you and hear your side."

She slammed the cupboard before stomping her way to us in the living room. "Tyler, that son-of-a bitch. He's such a tattle tale—I mean a liar. I would never ever do meth and I would never beat him. Do you know what is in that crap? His sister feeds him a bunch of bullshit, and he listens to her every damn time. He never listens to me, and I'm his mother for christ's sake. His father isn't any better. Who was it? Who made this false report? I'm pressing charges."

"No reason to get upset. We don't even know who called it in. But that individuals was concerned, so we're here to safety plan," I said.

Finney raised an eyebrow. "Safety plan?"

This was a new low for him, calling me out in front of a client. I held my tongue and stared at him to see if he had any better ideas.

He took a step forward, as if he was unable to process the idea of me doing a safety plan at the moment. I felt like an idiot, no doubt. Stupid social worker with a safety plan. I missed my friend. This guy standing before me was not him anymore. No, that man no longer existed.

"Let's work on a safety plan another day, okay?"

I nodded and took a step back.

"It's Molly, right?"

Molly rolled her eyes. "Yeah."

"Hi, I'm Deputy Finney. We're here to ask you a few questions. I met with Tyler at school today."

She jumped up with fire burning in her eyes and pointed her finger in his face. Finney did not move an inch. She startled me and I jumped, but he just kept eye contact with her.

"You don't talk to my boy without me there. That's illegal. I'll have you and your department sued. I know my rights."

He pushed her finger away. "I'm going to ask you to take a

step back. I'm here to talk with you, and ma'am, I will answer any and all questions you have. It's obvious you care about your son, and my job is to make sure he's safe, okay?"

His words were so caring and full of empathy.

"Then tell me why the hell you were talking to my son without my permission."

Finney pointed to the couch. "Have a seat, Ms. Eiler, and give me a chance to explain."

She sat down but she did not look happy about it. "Fine." She crossed her arms.

This was the most I'd gotten her to listen.

"I went there with a social worker."

She turned her head toward me and tapped her foot.

I was not lying for him. If he went there and spoke to the child without parental consent and without child protection there, that was on him.

"It wasn't me." I glanced at him, but he showed no disappointment when I did not cover for him.

"You're just like every other cop out there. You lied to me, and I will not let this go." She stood up.

"You're right, I didn't go there with Lyndsey, and it shows she isn't lying. But I did go there with a social worker named Tracey. She said she's worked with you before." He lifted an eyebrow at Molly.

She fell back on the couch, and I had to remind myself to close my mouth. Why would Tracey go to the school with him to meet with the kids on my case without even asking me? She was not on this case. I knew exactly why she did it. She wanted to work with Finney, of course. She wanted him back, and I'm sure it drove her crazy to know he was working a case with me.

My body burned with anger at the thought of the two of them being married. She couldn't wait to tell me about it when I first started working with her, and it hurt so bad that he married her. It wasn't until I heard they had been divorced that I finally felt a little better about it.

I would speak to my boss about Tracey's actions, because it was not okay that she went out and worked my case without letting me know. She was crossing the line and she had no right.

Molly's body suddenly relaxed. "Still not okay." Her voice was even calmer.

Finney surprised me. He did not talk down to her, and he was quite convincing.

"As a mother, your goal is to make sure your kids stay safe, right?"

Her hands were now in fists, covering her face. That was the calmest I'd ever seen her.

"Well, I mean, yeah."

He cleared his throat. "And my job is to make sure everyone is safe. It is also Tracey and Lyndsey's job to make sure children are safe."

Molly was speechless. I never thought anyone could make that woman speechless but he did it. She sadly nodded her head and listened intently to every word that came out of his mouth.

"There's no doubt in my mind that you love your children, Molly. And that's why I believe you'll be honest with us today so we can do our job and help your family."

She sat silent for a minute. "What do you want to know? I'm not a drug addict."

"I never said you were. But you do struggle with drugs. Don't you?"

She remained quiet, obviously thinking hard about whether or not she should answer his question truthfully.

"The pock marks on your face, the people in and out all hours of the night. If you don't get help, something serious could happen to your children. You don't want to get mixed up with drug dealers. I've seen what happens when they turn on people. And they will turn on you in a second to save themselves."

She stayed silent.

"I saw the bruise on Tyler's face. You didn't mean to hit him, did you?" His words came out in a soothing tone.

I glanced at Molly. She wiped away a tear with her hand. Finney had actually made Molly feel something ... a sense of remorse ... sadness ... regret?

The front door opened, and Tyler's smile turned into a frown when he saw us talking to his mother. The face of fear. The poor kid was scared to death about what was going to happen next.

Molly stood up, and her face hardened before our eyes. Her eyes were dark, and her jaw clenched. Her calm voice became a scream. She pointed her shaky finger at the sweet little boy. "You tell them you lied about me hitting you and doing drugs. I would never touch you and you know it! Is this what I get for always putting you first? You spoiled brat."

He stared at the ground.

"Tell them! Tell them I would never touch you!"

"She didn't hit me. I made it up," he said, under his breath.

I went over to him and led him outside while Finney stayed with Molly. I shut the door behind me as sobs escaped him.

"I told them she would get worse. They wouldn't listen. Why are you guys here? You don't know what it's like. You don't know what she's going to do to me when we're alone."

I kneeled down beside him on the porch. "Who, buddy? Who did you tell?"

"The lady and the police officer."

"Has she hit you before?"

He nodded.

"Do you feel safe going back into your house?" I needed him to tell me the way he felt. I needed to hear it in his own words to have any hope of getting a police hold.

He stared into my eyes, and I fought to hold back the tears. I felt broken right with him. He was scared to death, but I needed him to say it.

He shook his head.

"Tyler, buddy, it's okay. I will do everything to help you, so you don't get hurt anymore. Do you feel safe with your dad?"

He nodded.

"How about if I take you to him? Would you feel safer?"

He pursed his lips to hold back his cries. "What about my mom?"

"Your mom is sick, and she needs to get some help. I'm going to do everything I can to keep you safe so this doesn't happen again."

He stuck his pinky in the air. "Pinky swear?"

"Pinky swear," I said as our pinky's knotted together, and then released. "Now, wait here, I need to talk with the officer for a minute. He may have some questions for you, too. Do you think you can tell him the truth so he can help you?"

He nodded his head faster this time. "Then I can go see my dad?"

His words broke my heart. "Then you can go see your dad. Where is your sister? I'm surprised she isn't here with you."

"She missed the bus. She's probably at Jill's house. She does that a lot."

I gave him a hug, and he hugged me back. "Is Jill a friend of hers?"

He nodded again.

"Okay, let me talk to the officer really quick. I'll be right back. Wait here, okay?"

"Okay."

Finney was standing alone in the living room.

"She's in the bathroom," he said, pointing down the hall.

I stood a foot away so she could not overhear me.

"Tyler is scared to death of her. He wants to stay with his dad. The little girl is at a friend's house. I'll talk to her about signing a voluntary placement agreement so he can stay with his dad."

Finney's eyes locked with mine. "And if she doesn't?"

"Then I'm going to ask you to sign a seventy-two-hour police hold."

"I can do that."

The bathroom door opened, and I stood next to Finney as she came out.

"Molly, how would you feel about Tyler going to his dad's house?"

"Over my dead body—"

Finney took a step forward. "Tyler's safety is a priority right now, and we have to do what we believe is in the best interest of your son. I think it would be best for you to sign the paperwork to give yourself a chance to cool down."

"I didn't hit him, he's a liar. Kids make things up."

The truth was obvious, and we were all in the room when she practically admitted she hit him. Tyler's timing was not the best or we would have probably had a whole confession. Dang it.

"It's your call. We'd never make you do anything you didn't want to," I said.

"Take him, I don't give a shit. It's not illegal to discipline your child."

She tried to walk toward the front door. Finney stepped in front of her before she had a chance to reach her son.

"I have to take you into custody. Would you like to sign the voluntary before I cuff you?"

She glared at him and then me, and I was glad Finney was

there because just her look was terrifying. I knew what she was capable of.

"Do I have a choice?"

She put her hand out for the papers. I reached into my bag and grabbed the paperwork. She signed it and threw it on the floor.

Finney leaned close to my ear. "Why don't you get him out of here before I arrest her. He doesn't need to see this or hear what she has to say. I have a feeling she isn't going without a fight."

I nodded and he held out his arm to prevent me from picking up the paperwork on the floor. Instead, he picked it up and handed it to me with a nod.

I took Tyler to his father's house and gave his father the rundown. Finney sent a text to me that a search warrant was being filed so they could search her house for drugs. He was hoping the charges would stick and her bail would be set high enough where she would not be able to pay it and get released too soon.

*Then*

Of course, my brother was in the kitchen when I got home, and my soaking wet clothes hugged my body. I tried to walk on my tiptoes, so I would not drench the floor.

Brad raised an eyebrow. "You know most people put on a swimsuit before jumping in the water, right?"

"Thanks, brainiac, I'll take note of that for next time."

"Dad's at work and mom is laying down, so you should be safe if you don't want to answer any questions as to why your clothes are sopping wet."

He was right, my parents would be angry and would probably make me stay in if they saw my clothes. They would ask way too many questions. Sometimes Brad could be such a jerk one minute and such a good brother the next.

I jumped in the shower and warmed up, and hung my clothes in the shower to dry once I got out. I was in my room, trying to find my favorite sweatshirt when I heard a tap on my window. I moved the curtain to peek outside into the dark.

Kevin was standing on the driveway and smirking at me. He wound up and threw what sounded like a pebble at my window. It bounced off and made a light sound. I pushed open my window.

"What are you doing? My dad would kill you if he sees you throwing rocks at my window."

"Your dad loves me. Going to the door is overrated."

True. "You're lucky he isn't here then. What do you want?"

"I just started a fire. Come have some s'mores and hang out with me. You're taking too long. What are you doing, putting on makeup?"

I shook my head. "I needed a shower to warm up. I told you I'd be right over. Just give me a minute, Romeo."

"What did you need a shower for? The fire will warm you up."

"Give me a second. I'll be right there, okay?"

I pulled back my hair so it would look less wet and found my sweatshirt as I walked through the house. My mom stood behind an ironing board with my dad's uniforms while watching Beverly Hills 90210. She stopped to acknowledge me. "Where are you going, sweetie?"

"To a bonfire next door with Kevin."

She stood up straight and her face scrunched up. A mom lecture was coming on.

"Don't you think you may be spending a little too much time with Kevin?"

"Mom, he's my friend."

She walked closer and tucked my hair behind my ear like I was ten. I let her because I wanted to go.

"Do you think maybe we should be having the sex talk?"

"I'm sixteen years old, mom. Just let me go. We'll be out by the fire the whole time, I promise."

She hesitated, which was a good sign.

"Okay, but be careful. You aren't drinking over there are you?"

"Dad would smell it on my breath the minute I got home. No, we aren't drinking."

She put her hand on my shoulder and guided me out the door. "Eleven o'clock at the latest."

"Thanks, mom." I kissed her on the cheek before she could change her mind.

Kevin was poking at the fire when I walked up. As soon as our eyes met, a huge grin spread across his face, which gave me instant goosebumps up my arms.

"I was thinking I was going to be hanging out by the fire all by myself."

I sat down in the plastic chair in front of the fire. "It's been like five minutes since you were throwing rocks at my windows. Learn some patience. Aren't Ethan and Kat coming?"

"They aren't answering my calls. I don't know what is going on with them. I guess they really hit it off, huh?"

"Looked like it. What do you think of Ethan?"

"I like him. He's like my long-lost brother."

"And Kat?"

He put a marshmallow on his stick. "She's great. I think they will be good together."

"Me too. As long as her mom doesn't find out. She's strict and doesn't want Kat hanging around boys."

He laughed, "She's what, seventeen years old? Does her mother think she has that kind of control?"

"I guess. I don't know, she's weird. I have a feeling they went to Kat's house because her mom is out tonight with the

Side Lake ladies. We probably have some time before they show up. While we're waiting, why don't you tell me about yourself. What are your parents like?"

"What do you want to know?"

Trying to get information about his parents was like pulling teeth. I met them a few times, but they were gone a lot, and when they were there, his father hid out in his office and his mother always seemed to be cooking. She obviously liked to keep busy and be a normal mother, just with the doctor's title.

"What are they like? Are they strict? Do you get along? Your mom seems nice. I like her."

"My life isn't really that exciting. They're busy all the time being doctors, so Troy has pretty much raised me. You already know that though."

I nodded, not wanting to stop him from telling me more. I met his brother, Troy, a few times. He was much nicer than my brother, even though he and my brother were good friends.

"My dad isn't exactly the nicest guy. He was in the military when he was younger, so everything about him is very pro-military. As long as we chip in and clean up and answer, yes, sir, he's alright."

"What's it like when he's not alright?"

He pulled up his sleeve and showed me a three-inch scar. "It looks like this. When I was ten, he held my arm down on the stove. And when I was twelve, I didn't have the dishes done and he did this," he said pulling up his other sleeve to reveal another scar. "This was a lighter."

"Oh my gosh, Kevin, I had no idea."

"Yeah. Things were pretty bad for a while. He's much better now, since he found out he's dying."

I gasped. "Is he really dying?"

He leaned forward, staring into the fire. "Yeah, he has pancreatic cancer. It's pretty aggressive."

"I'm so sorry."

He brushed me off with a wave of his hand.

"Don't be. He pretends it isn't happening. He doesn't really talk about it. After his diagnosis, he said when it's his time, it's his time. I think he'd rather be with patients than take the time to get chemo or whatever."

I had to ask, "Is it terminal?"

"Yeah, although he doesn't talk about it so I'm not sure how long they think he will live. He's on a special diet, and I think he's on some pills, something his doctor prescribed. I'm not sure what they are for exactly. I know he was talking about some experimental drugs or something. He's weak and some days he can hardly walk. He doesn't hit me anymore. Plus, I'm big enough to take him on so he hasn't hit me in a few years."

I never would have guessed there was trouble in Kevin's home the way he radiated confidence and seemed so carefree. This was not easy for him to talk about, so I changed the subject. "Well, if you ever want to talk about it, I'm always here. Night or day, okay?"

He nodded.

"Should we spy on Ethan and Kat? They did ditch us, so it's well deserved. We should try her gazebo out back. That's where Kat and I usually hang out at her house."

"I love the way you think."

Kevin put out the fire, and a smile spread across his face before he said, "You think we'll catch them getting it on?"

"Yeah, probably but too bad for them. I'm sure she's losing her virginity as we speak."

He put his arm around my shoulder. "They haven't been together very long."

76

"But she seemed ready when I talked to her. I think a part of her wants to punish her mom by being self-destructive. I can't really talk her out of it. She'll learn on her own."

"You sound like you're much older than you are."

I looked down, avoiding his eyes. "I hear that a lot. I'm too responsible sometimes. It's my best and worst quality. Drives Kat crazy."

"I think it's awesome."

"You do?"

"I do. It's easy to make impulsive choices at our age. You know, our brains aren't fully formed yet. Seems like yours already is."

I grinned to myself. No one ever complimented me on my uptight, overthinking nature. Well, no one my age. He got who I was, and he was not trying to change me.

We walked down Turtle Creek Road and turned onto Kat's long driveway. Her house was out on a peninsula in a world of its own. Their house was the nicest one on Turtle Creek, with the most beautiful view of the water.

Kevin turned to me. "Could Kat's parents be home yet? Do they park in the driveway?"

"Her dad passed away years ago so it's just her mom. I think she went to Bimbos with some of the Side Lake ladies. They like to get together and have pizza and wings a couple times a year. She always parks her car in the driveway in the summer. She only parks in the garage when the weather is bad."

The darkness hid the house's beautiful exterior until we got close enough that the motion light turned on. Moving lights shone on us from behind as someone turned into the driveway.

We both turned to look behind us.

"Oh, no. It's Kat's mom! We need to find them quick. Run!"

The driveway was long, which was a good thing. "We may have enough time to grab them before she catches Ethan with Kat."

The grass crunched beneath Kevin's feet behind me. He was passing me. We rounded the house on the east side.

"The gazebo!" I said, and pointed. "The door is on the other side." I was out of breath, my heart pounding in my chest. If Kat's mother caught her, who knows what she'd do. She was strict and mean all the time. She believed sex before marriage was not acceptable.

He leaped up the three steps and threw open the door. I panted and leaned over to try to catch my breath.

Kat squealed. "Get out!"

"Your mom is home. Get your damn clothes on," Kevin said.

The bright light flipped on and blinded me.

I heard Kat's voice cry out. "Not the light, you idiot. She'll know where we are."

I heard a sliding door, and I knew they were in trouble. Kevin got out just in time as the shadow of her mom entered the gazebo from the other side.

Kevin waved me to follow as he ducked. We ran for our lives around the house and past the two garages. I could hear her mother yelling, but her words were unclear from this far away.

Our feet hit the driveway's pavement, and I ran as fast as my legs would let me. My adrenaline carried me without even feeling out of breath. Once Kevin reached the road, he slowed down to a fast walk.

I stopped running and struggled to catch my breath. Kevin's gasped for air loud and sporadically. His breaths turned into loud breaths of laughter. I laughed with him. I lay down on the grass by my driveway and put my hands on my stomach as it bounced out of control. He fell to the ground next to me. It felt like forever before we stopped laughing.

I rolled over on my left side, and he turned onto his right. The moonlight shone down on him enough to see his silhouette. "Were they completely naked?"

Although I did not want to see it in person, I needed to know how much trouble Kat was in.

"They hadn't found their underwear by the time her mom opened the door. I saw the look on her face, and I was gone. No way she saw me."

"She'd think you were having a three-some!"

I could not tell for sure, but it looked like he was smiling in the dark.

"Just what I need her to tell my mom. How would I explain that?"

"Luckily you don't have to. I'm really glad I'm not Kat right now."

We both lay there in silence. Exhaustion hit me now that the adrenaline rush was gone.

"Kat was literally on top of him on that couch when I walked in. I didn't see anything, though. She covered herself up right away with a pillow, and I turned around. See, I'm a gentleman."

I shook my head.

"It can't be—" My words were cut off by the pounding of feet.

We both jumped up and watched as Ethan ran in the opposite direction from the driveway.

Kevin yelled after him. "Ethan, Ethan, wait!"

Ethan looked behind as he ran and turned around, as if he thought he was imagining someone calling out his name. He stopped then kept walking in the opposite direction.

"Ethan, it's Kevin. Over here!"

He did a one eighty and charged at us like he was going to take Kevin out, but he ran right past us and down my driveway. He reached my house and collapsed on the steps, panting heavily.

"That was horrible."

I put my fist over my mouth. "What happened?"

"She threw pillows at me!" He was pulling on his hair.

"Pillows?" Kevin and I said at the same time. We turned our heads to look at each other.

"Yeah, pillows. Her mom told me to get the hell out, and she threw pillows at me." He looked up at me. "Do you think Kat is going to be okay? I know she talks about her mom being overprotective, but she was just plain crazy."

"You'd probably feel the same way if your daughter was getting it on with some strange guy in your house. A guy she only met ..."

His head was now between his knees as he cut me off. "What was I thinking? We weren't even ready to have sex. She was so insistent."

Kevin laughed. "Thinking with your hormones, buddy."

I hit him in the shoulder.

"What?"

"You aren't helping," I said. "Do you guys want to come inside?"

Ethan stood up, looking dazed and confused. "I better go home. Let me know the minute you hear anything."

"I will."

Kevin squeezed my shoulder and turned back to Ethan. "I'll walk you."

I stood alone in the dark after they left, staring up at the stars in the sky. Kat and Ethan were moving too fast. She was back after being sent away for the entire summer. Did she think this through? Her mother could send her back to the

Cities, and I would lose her again. The gazebo out back was connected to her house by a sliding glass door. Did she want to get caught? But that was a stupid thought. Why would she want to get caught? Did she realize her mother could come home at any time?

*Now*

"Kat, I think you should consider breaking your rule and come up for Troy and Victoria's wedding. Don't you want to see Ethan?"

"I won't step foot in Side Lake unless my mother suddenly disappears, and I don't want to see Ethan."

"It's been years since you last saw him, come on. Plus, you said it yourself, your mom doesn't leave her house. It's not like she will be at the wedding. I'm sure she still doesn't like Ethan and if she does show up, I'll run her out for you."

Her nervous laughter broke through the phone call. "I know you would, but I think you should think about coming to visit me instead."

I opened the door to my porch and let the wind blow my hair. "I wish I could. I promise I'll come see you as soon as I can. I miss you. It's been forever."

"I know. I'd love to see what Kevin looks like now. I wonder if I'd even recognize him."

"You'd recognize him, but he's filled out. In a good way. I just wish he was the same person he used to be. We don't talk about anything other than the case we're working together."

Kat hated what happened between Finney and me. She always thought we would end up together, but the joke was on her. I could not imagine us together now. He was not the same person he used to be.

After the morning meeting, I called Kevin to let him know I planned to see Molly. She had been released from custody after posting bond. I was disappointed they did not put her on supervised release or something. What if she showed up at her ex-husband's house demanding to get her kids back? In my experience, Tyler did not have a backbone, and I had the feeling he was still in love with Molly.

Finney answered on the first ring.

"Deputy Finney."

"Hi, uh, it's Lyndsey calling. I wanted you to know I'm going to see Molly. I heard she was released on bond."

"Yes she was. She's at home. You planning on stopping by?"

"Yeah, sometime this morning. I wasn't sure if you were still working on your investigation, so I thought I'd call and see if you wanted to go along."

"I'm still working on my investigation. I should be able to make it over there this morning. Are you worried she'll try to take the kids from the dad's house?"

The fear in Tyler's eyes circled in my head. Sometimes I wondered why I even tried. Finney did not see the fear in the kid's eyes like I did when he was out on the deck with me.

I took a deep breath. "Well, she did sign that voluntary, so if she tries to take him back I could always put out a police hold." I paused. "Although something bad would have to happen for it to be imminent danger where we could actually do a police hold today. Even if you agree."

"Let's hope she doesn't try to take him. Can she do that?"

"Technically she needs to give me twenty-four hours' notice before she can take him back, but yeah, without a hold or a pre-petition screening, she can."

He groaned. "Okay, how long until you go over there?"

I looked at my watch. "Probably about an hour."

"I'll meet you there as long as I don't get called out on an emergency. Give me a call on your way there, and I'll do what I can to make it there."

"Okay, thanks."

After I got off the phone, I took out her file and did some time recording and documentation. I looked at some of the previous allegations against her. A long list of child endangerment and neglect was recorded, but what looked like only one determination. After an investigation is completed, a determination is made when there is enough proof to determine the parent is guilty of an allegation. When they get a background check it would show up if they were applying for a job working with children or vulnerable adults.

Tracey came up to my cubicle, and although I wanted to pretend I was too busy to notice her, she cleared her throat so I looked over at her. Her arms were crossed and her nose was slightly up in the air. She flipped her hair behind her shoulder.

"I heard about Molly Eiler, and I think I would be the best person for this case. She likes me a lot more, and not to be rude or anything, but people are always complaining about what a crappy social worker you are, and I know Kevin isn't really a fan of yours."

I clenched my teeth and held my tongue. I wanted to tell her off for seeing the kids on my case without talking to me first. But I held back because I would not get anywhere, and I would not stoop to her level.

"I think I've got it, but thanks anyway," I said.

"Um, sure you do. I hope you don't screw up this investigation for Kevin. I'm meeting him for drinks after work. I think he wants to get back together." She smiled and lifted her nose in the air.

My face fell before I caught myself, and by the look in her eyes she knew she got to me. That was exactly what she wanted.

"Oh, you don't still have a thing for him, do you?" She tapped me on my shoulder. I stared at her hand. "You poor thing. I can't believe you're still hung up on him. That's so cute. He never liked you that way. That's why he married me."

And divorced you, I wanted to say.

She walked away with extra emphasis on her hips as she took each step. She was a horrible person. Finney would never believe I had a crush on him. Would he? I guess I would soon find out. If only he would stop pretending he had no idea who I was, or that I was just another social worker to him. He was driving me crazy.


Molly's car was in her driveway and Kevin was not picking up his phone. The front door was open, and I could see into her house from the screen door. She was passed out on her couch with a bottle of vodka at her feet and a half full lowball glass in her hand. I knocked with my knuckles, but she did not move. I knocked again, louder, and she jumped a foot off the couch. She looked around and then our eyes locked. If she could kill me with a look, I'd be dead already. She put her glass down on the floor and waved me in.

Something did not feel right. The hairs on the back of my neck stood up, and I fought the feeling that something felt a bit off. Maybe I was overreacting. I shook off the feeling.

"Hey, Molly. How are you doing?"

She was moving in slow motion when she picked up something from the floor and threw it at me. It shattered on the wall behind me.

"Get the hell out of my house, you stupid bitch. You're ruining my life!"

I don't think I've ever moved so fast. As I flew down the porch steps, she threw her lowball glass at me. It broke right next to my leg. I climbed into the silver county car, and that's when she grabbed the baseball bat, threw it over her shoulder, and charged me. I tried to shift my car into reverse, but it would not budge. What the hell was going on? My fight or flight response kicked into overdrive and my heart felt like it would beat out of my chest. My hands shook, and I lost my hearing as she charged toward my window.

I put my hands over my head to protect it, and waited for the blow to shatter my window, but it did not come. The baseball bat went flying onto the sidewalk. I had no idea how or why until I saw a man in uniform cuffing her behind her back.

Kevin. He walked her over to his squad and put her in the back seat and shut the door. At that moment, I lost all control and broke down in my car, crying into my steering wheel. This was something I was not prepared for, something I never saw coming.

The knock on my window made me jump. Kevin looked at me with sadness in his eyes.

I rolled down the window, unwilling to open my door or get out of the car. I could hardly get my hands to move to the button, but somehow, I did.

He bent down to look at me. "Are you okay?"

I shook my head. The tears kept coming. "I ... need to get out of here."

He swiped his thumb under my eyes twice to wipe away the tears, and then he squeezed my shoulder.

He looked over the car. Another squad car was pulling up.

"I'll be right back, okay? I'll have this sheriff book her in. Don't drive away, okay? It's not safe when you're feeling this way. You need to calm down first."

All I wanted to do was get as far away from this place as I could, but for some reason I still trusted him.

"Promise me?"

I nodded, but I could not figure out how to speak. My chin quivered.

He palmed my chin and lifted my head. I stared into his eyes for just a second until he walked away. I saw the old Kevin in his eyes, and I wanted to wrap my arms around him. I wanted to feel safe in his arms.

They put Molly into the other squad, and it drove away. Kevin came back to my window.

"How are you doing?"

I stumbled my words, unsure of how to answer that.

He hung his head. "I'm sorry I wasn't here. I wish you had waited for me."

His stone-cold look was now replaced with a droopy face.

I shook out my arms and cleared my throat. "I'm ready to leave."

"You feel okay to drive?

I nodded.

He looked as though he was unsure whether or not he should let me drive. "Okay, I'll follow you. Where are you planning on going? Were you hurt at all?"

"No. She missed me. I'm not sure where I'm going. Anywhere away from here."

He squinted at me and reached his hand behind my head. His hand came away covered in blood.

"Why don't you ride with me? Someone can pick up the car or the county can tow it. You need to go to the hospital, you're bleeding." His voice was steady, but his eyebrows drew together and his eyes drooped.

I reached back and felt a sting on my head from my touch. My hand was sticky with blood when I pulled it away. I stared at it and the whole world went dark.

## *Then*

～

A week went by before Kat was let out of her house. She showed up on my doorstep with dark circles under her eyes, and her low-cut tank tops were replaced with an oversized sweatshirt.

I did not say a word. Instead, I wrapped my arms around her. Her body was stiff at first, then she relaxed into my arms and finally collapsed.

"Oh, honey, how are you?"

She was trying as hard as she could not to lose it. "Can we talk about something else?"

"Of course. I'm here whenever you're ready."

She nodded, her eyes filling with tears. "Thank you."

"Should we see if my dad will take us waterskiing?"

"Yes, that would be wonderful."

When we got back, the sun was setting. Even with sunburns, chapped lips, and sore forearms, we were full of energy. I missed my friend. Having her smiling at me was so great. That's what the lake did for us. Her frown was gone and although she still looked tired, she had more color in her skin than earlier. The warm sun on our skin, the water under our feet, and the cool breeze as we cruised around the chain of lakes was meditating and relaxing.

Every time we passed a boat while going through the channels, we'd wave with big smiles, and squint to see if we recognized the boaters, and they would do the same. Side Lake people were the friendliest people. Even people who weren't from Side Lake but were on the chain turned into friendly faces.

Maybe the friendliness came from finally being able to spend days at the lake under the hot sun after months of sub below temperatures that kept us in our houses all day.

We went to Little Sturgeon Lake when we wanted to ski because there were fewer people, and Big Sturgeon when we wanted to tube or just cruise around. Sometimes we would cabin hop and visit our friends. If someone on the boat knew someone, we'd stop in, tie up our boat and visit.

A lot of summer people only came to their cabins on the weekends from Memorial Day to Labor Day. Many of them lived in the Cities. Some took the summers off from their busy jobs or worked remote as they enjoyed a Side Lake summer. A lot of people from the Cities had cabins up north somewhere to escape the busy lives of St. Paul and Minneapolis. With rush hour traffic, demanding jobs, and the busyness of their big city lives, people liked to relax at the lake.

Our house belonged to our family for three generations, so we did not have to be rich to buy it, but lake shore taxes were crazy expensive. Finding the money to afford living on the lake was sometimes a struggle for my parents. Sure, they did well financially, but we were not rich. Not like the Finneys or Kat's mother. Although money never got in the way of our friendship, because we all belonged here. We were Sidelakers and Sidelakers stuck together.

We laid on our towels on the dock. The wood was uncomfortable beneath our bodies, but we did not care as we gazed up at the stars.

"I'm surprised we didn't see Kevin today," Kat said, without moving her head to look at me.

"I sent him a text earlier and told him not to bug us because we needed our girl time."

Now she sat up. "You did not! You really do love me. Was he pissed?"

"I did, I do, and no, he was not pissed. He understood."

She laid back down. "Because he looooves you. So, do you like like Kevin?"

"Like, like, huh?" I knew what she was getting at, and I definitely had a crush, but once I admitted it, our friendship would become awkward.

"I think he's hot and I have a crush on him, but I don't want anything more than that because we'll break up one day and our friendship would be shot and—"

"Calm down. It was just a question."

Yeah, a question I could not answer because I was head over heels in love with him. Every day we spent together, I fell harder. When he taught me how to kayak, kicked my butt at tennis without trying, the way he cared so deeply, and always saw the beauty in everything all around him. I liked him so much it hurt, and the thought of him going back to Duluth and not being next door killed me.

But I could not tell Kat all that, she'd make fun of me. I never fell for guys. She was the one who fell for guys five minutes after meeting them. We had both changed a lot this summer.

"I'm sorry, I didn't realize you liked him so much."

I groaned.

"So, have you hung out with Ethan ... since ... you know."

"Since your mom walked in on you having sex with him and forbid you from leaving your house, you mean? No."

I waited for her to yell at me, but nothing came. She was silent for a minute.

"It was horrible. I'm almost an adult, for Pete's sake. I was so embarrassed. I wouldn't be surprised if Ethan never spoke to me again."

"It's not your fault. He knew there was a possibility your mom could come home. He took that risk. If he stops talking to you for that, then he's a jerk."

"I guess. But I can't get the look on my mother's face out of my head. I've never seen her so pissed. Her perfect daughter dared to have sex. I can't even get a bad grade on my report card without her sending me away."

I sat up because this was not a conversation I could have with her while staring at the sky.

"Are you okay?"

She sat up, too, hugging her knees and looking out into the dark water. "I can't wait until I move out. She's ruining my life. She doesn't understand what it's like to be a teen anymore." She paused, deep in thought. "Can you do me a favor?"

"Whatever you need."

"Will you give Ethan this letter?" She put a piece of paper in my palm.

"I can do that. Do you really think your mom isn't going to let you see him again?"

She shrugged. "I don't know. You know how she is. I'm surprised she even agreed to let me come here."

"Kat!"

My mother called from the deck on my house.

"What, mom?" I yelled back.

"Kat's mom is here."

"Of course she is. Please give him that letter, okay? My mom took my phone, so I have no way to reach him. This letter will explain everything. Please don't read it, okay? It's better you don't know what's in it."

She walked away, and I stared at the sealed envelope. I would be lying if I said I wasn't curious. I wanted to open it so much, but instead I walked over to Pine Beach before the temptation had me curious enough to break my promise to my best friend.

I knocked on the door of his motorhome.

Ethan smiled at me when he opened the door. He glanced over my shoulder, as if Kat was hiding somewhere in the trees.

"What's up, Lyndsey?"

"I thought you might want to know Kat's mom finally let her out of the house, and we spent the day boating."

He shut the door behind him, and we walked away from his house so his parents would not overhear.

"How is she?"

"About as good as expected after her mom caught her naked and having sex in the gazebo with a random boy."

He looked away, his face red. "I bet Kat hates me now, huh?"

"You both said the same thing. She doesn't hate you. The exact opposite, I think. I don't know, she really didn't talk much about it. She wanted me to deliver this letter to you."

He held it in his hand as if it was a bomb.

"Don't open it while I'm around. I had strict instructions not to read it, and I don't intend to break my promise."

I really wanted to read that letter. A part of me wanted to let him open it just so I could look over his shoulder, but I needed to be a good friend. She'd tell me later anyway, or so I hoped.

"You're a good friend, you know that?"

I waved him off. "Yeah, yeah. I really hope you aren't a player. She'd be devastated if she lost you."

"I'm not a player. I think I love her. She was my first, you know."

I was definitely surprised, but I believed him for some reason. "And you were hers."

"Really?"

"You two really need to talk more. Anyway, I better get home. Kevin and I are going kayaking tomorrow morning if you want to come. You'd need to bring your own kayak though, he only has two."

He nodded, staring at the letter in his hands. "I could use a distraction, thank you. I can't get her and what happened out of my mind."

"I can't imagine," I said, before turning to walk away.

"Lyndsey, you're a good friend, you know that? Kat is lucky to have you."

"You owe me," I said, in a teasing voice. "Be good to my friend." If her mother ever let them see each other again, that is.

His somber look told me he knew that was a possibility as well. Kat's mother was not what we called easy going, but she loved Kat.

As summer turned to fall and the boats were taken off the lakes and the docks pulled in for the winter, I saw less and less of Kat. Her mother pulled her out of school, and she was being home schooled. I also saw less of Ethan. He never did show up kayaking that morning, and he stopped answering both Kevin and my texts.

. . .

At first, Kat came over a couple times a week, and then she never came over until early November.

The week after Halloween, and the day after the first snowfall of the year, I went out on the deck to breathe in the fresh, cold air, with my cup of hot cocoa. Kat was standing by the shore right where the dock usually stood, but was now put away until the spring. She was staring at the water. Her shoulders were trembling, and her face was in her hands.

I raced to her side and cradled her head in my arms. "What's wrong?"

"Please ... don't make me ... talk. Just let me cry."

"Whatever you need," I whispered in her ear. "I'm here for you." I ran my fingers through her hair with one hand.

After quite some time, her tears dried up and she stopped crying. "I'm moving to the Cites."

I blinked. "What? Is your mom still that upset about—"

"No, I just need to get away from her for a while, you know. It was my idea."

I knew Kat better than anyone. She was either lying or hiding something. I dared not push her. She would tell me when she was ready.

"I'm going to miss you so much. We'll still be best friends forever and always."

She nodded. "If Kevin replaces me, I'm going to kick his butt."

"There's no competition. You're my person."


She did come back, but we never lost contact. The longer she stayed away, the more certain she felt that she never wanted to return. She did not visit. She said she just couldn't. I did not push, and she never told me much about it. I knew one day when she was ready, she would open up to me and maybe she would come home.

# Now

When I came to, Kevin was sitting at my bedside, his hand holding mine. He looked at me with such tenderness, like he had as a teenager. His eyes were now so gentle and his smile so sweet. The back of his hand rubbed my face with such tenderness.

"Wh-where am I?" But the bed, the light green walls and equipment in the room gave it away.

He leaned forward. "You are in the hospital. You have a little bump on your head. Doc had to give you fifteen stitches. A piece of glass must have hit you in the back of the head when Molly threw that bottle at the wall."

I touched the burning spot on the back of my head and felt a bandage in my hair. My hair was spiky and short in the spot underneath the dressing.

"Did they shave my head?"

He laughed. "Just a little spot. They said your longer hair would hide it. More importantly, you had a concussion."

I sat up. "I need to call my boss." I looked around for my cell phone.

He touched my hand and sent tingles throughout my

body. My eyes met his, and I wondered if he felt it, too. But maybe the meds made me feel that way. I could only hope. Did he feel it, too?

"Don't worry, I called Tracey and told her to let your supervisor know."

"You have got to be kidding me! Tracey?" Why Tracey? He did hate me or maybe he had a thing for her again? I had a hard time keeping up. Unless he really did want to get back together with her. Didn't they separate for a reason? I used to know every secret he had, but I no longer knew a thing about him. Did he know I knew he married her? And divorced her? Our desks are in cubicles, and I overheard Hannah talking about the divorce one day. I was pretty sure I almost had a heart attack that day.

"You still don't like Tracey? But you two work together now."

He always was clueless when it came to Tracey. Just because we worked together did not mean we liked each other. If he married her, how would he not know she carried a grudge? Although they divorced so maybe he found out.

"Never mind." I forgot they were going out for drinks that night. She made sure to tell me. He probably had to call and cancel their date.

An awkward silence rested between us. I closed my eyes to escape, without having to strike up a conversation.

"You really had me worried, you know?"

"That's funny. Just a few days ago you acted like you didn't even know who I was."

He clasped his hands in his lap and stared down.

"I—"

I did not want to hear it. I didn't want to know. "Listen, my head really hurts. Thank you for getting me here, but I'm okay, really?"

Why did the hurt look in his eyes make me feel guilty?

"I understand. I'm sorry for the way I acted. I'd never forget you. You know that. Is there someone I can call to be here with you then?"

"I can call someone. Hand me my phone."

The next day I woke up in the comfort of my own bed. Kevin did not leave my side until Maddy came to the hospital to take his place. The hospital let me go before the end of the day. She got Brad to lug over the playpen so David could sleep right beside us in my room, and Maddy slept next to me all night.

The next morning, we walked onto the patio while David was still sleeping sound. The day was sunny and beautiful.

"I can't believe she attacked you!"

Maddy was in disbelief after I told her the story.

"I can't believe she threw a bottle of alcohol at you."

"I can't say I'm surprised, to be honest. I'm more surprised she wasted what was left of the bottle by throwing it at me. Have I told you I hate my job?"

She put her hand on my shoulder before sitting next to me on the deck. "You're always worrying about everyone else, you never have any time for you. Your job is the worst for that. You give it all you have and now look at you. Stitches. A shaved head. What's next? I'm worried about you."

"I don't know," I answered her honestly.

The deck was the only place where I could destress. Something about the calmness of the lake, the small waves, and the wind blowing my hair back calmed me. The people in the boats that passed by waved, and I smiled and waved back. I did not know everyone on the lake even though I'd lived here my whole life, but sometimes it felt that way.

She took the cup of coffee I poured her. "What are you going to do about work?"

"I'm going to ask for paid time off so I can heal both physically and mentally."

"That makes me feel so much better. It's also good for you and for me."

I scrunched my nose.

"We can go boating and have some bonfires, and if we're feeling brave, we can put on our wet suits and go skiing. Whitney will be so glad you'll be around more." Whitney was a good friend of Maddy's that lived in Side Lake and was a teacher at the school with Maddy.

I took a sip of my wine. "I'm in."

But I could not seem to get the incident off my mind. What if Molly had hit me with the bottle and knocked me out? She could have killed me. Would I be ready to go back to work in a month? Would I want to?

As a social worker, just taking a couple days off was a challenge. What if my cases blew up? Who would cover? What if someone tried calling me due to an emergency?

Maddy looked at me as if she could read my thoughts. "What's on your mind?"

"Just everything. I love helping people through the darkest times in their life, but sometimes I feel like it's killing me."

I heard the loons in the distance and thought about Kevin and the story he told me about the way they moved in the water. How they swam like submarines beneath the surface of the water, where we could not see them moving. I had a hard time getting him off my mind. He was the reason I fell in love with the lake and mother nature. I used to feel so stuck as a child until I met him. He had this way of making me feel things I'd never felt before. I thought that Kevin was gone, but he sat by my bedside when I was hurt and wouldn't leave my side until I made him. I saw that guy I once knew in his expression, but was it just his guilt for not being there to prevent the whole incident with Molly?

. . .

Maddy and David went home late in the morning. She wanted to stay, but I kicked her out with promises that I would keep checking in with her and I'd be all right.

I wandered the house, but I felt sick to my stomach. The pressure of everything, and everyone. I felt so alone for the first time, sitting on the porch with my glass of water, instead of wine.

My doorbell rang. Maddy never rang the doorbell. Who else could it be?

I opened the door and stood there frozen.

Those perfect brown eyes stared back at me. He was looking down, but he looked up when I answered the door and our eyes met.

Neither of us said anything. We both just stared at each other until he ran his hand through his perfect hair.

"Finney," I said. I'm not sure why it came out the way it did, but I couldn't hide my surprise.

"Can I come in?"

I shook my head, coming back to the present. "Yeah, come in."

He walked past me and looked around. "This place hasn't changed since we were kids. It almost feels like I'm home."

I shut the door and followed him into the living room. What exactly did he mean by that?

"What are you doing here?"

"Can I sit?"

The way he said it, he was asking me if being there was okay. If he was welcome in my home.

"Yes, sit wherever."

Silence.

He sat down. I did the same, but I was unsure of where to put my hands so I sat on them. I sat on the recliner across from him because sitting next to him on the couch would just be too weird.

"Why are you here?" That did not come out of my mouth the same way it did in my head.

"I wanted to make sure you were okay. Tracey said you were taking some time off."

"Tracey, of course."

I rolled my eyes like a teenage girl. Even the sound of her name was enough to make my skin crawl. "I need some time, that's all."

He nodded with understanding and sadness in his eyes. "I'm sorry I wasn't there."

That's what this was about. He felt guilty for not being there.

"It's not your fault. Molly has never done anything like that before. I had this feeling before I went inside her house though ... I should have known."

He leaned forward, his hands fidgeting. His posture was so perfect, and his body radiated confidence. I found it hard to believe this was the same Kevin I knew inside and out not too long ago. Now I had a hard time looking at him without blushing. He was so damn good looking and I ... well, had I changed at all?

"I can't stop thinking about it. I would never have forgiven myself if something happened to you."

Was this the same guy who ignored me when I saw him, who hated me in college and gave up on our friendship? The one who abandoned me for my worst enemy and then married her? He did not even see it. He never did. Tracey was the evilest person I'd ever met, and he was still blinded by her.

"I didn't realize you cared." My words were cold, but he deserved it.

He put his fist in front of his mouth, and chose his words carefully. "Is that really what you think?"

What could I say to that? Of course, that is what I thought.

He cleared his throat, understanding my silence was a yes. "I've been an asshole and I'm sorry."

I nodded and blinked away the tears. He had no idea how much I loved him. But I gave up on him long ago. How long until he went back to being the grumpy guy? When he stopped feeling guilty?

"Listen, I'm taking some vacation myself. Can we hang out tomorrow? Sit and talk? I feel awful."

I hated that I still felt this connection with him. I wanted to jump into his arms and forget what he did. I wanted to erase our past and move forward, but I knew he'd break my heart again.

"I don't know. I think I need some time. I think you should go."

He nodded and stood up, but his feet dragged as he made for the door. He turned around and caught me off guard. Our faces were just a few inches apart. I took a step back, but what I really wanted to do was lean forward.

I needed some time to think. What should I say to him? I did not blame him for what happened. He saved my life by stopping her with that bat. I should not have gone into that house alone, but why does he now want to hang out, as he called it? We grew apart long ago.

"Are you going to my brother's wedding this weekend?"

If I hadn't already RSVP'd, I would have said no. He probably knew I was going. Why did he care?

"Yeah."

"Good. I'll see you there."

I nodded but I would be staying as far away from him as possible. Who needed his pity friendship. I had friends. Well, I had Maddy and Kat and my family. I did not need him.

*Then*

By the summer before my senior year, I was dying to see Kevin. We texted often, and I even met him in Duluth a few times for rock climbing and to see a play or a couple of movies. But the summer was what truly mattered.

Our summers in Side Lake were when we really clicked, and when we spent every day together.

I spent the school year applying for colleges and researching what I wanted to major in. I was still undecided. Kevin was still trying to talk me into law enforcement school.

Kat's texts and calls became fewer and farther between now that she was living across the state.

Then summer arrived, and Kevin and I became more inseparable than ever. My goal was to make him see me as more than a friend. I bought a new swimsuit that showed off a little more cleavage and a bright pink suit with white polka dots that made my skin look tanned, even though I slathered myself with sunscreen every time I stepped outside. I was light skinned and burned easily.

My father dropped Kevin and I off at McCarthy's beach at

eleven o'clock in the morning on a Saturday. The beach was already half full. We found a nice place to lay out our towels in the middle of the sand. Normally when we came as a family, we would find a more secluded spot under the trees to hide from the crowds, but Kevin and I wanted to see people our age.

I could only imagine what my friends from school would think seeing me there with Kevin. His confidence and the way he smiled at anyone who made eye contact with him made him even more attractive. I was proud to be the woman on his shoulder, if only we were more than friends.

He took off his shirt and threw it on top of his backpack. He pulled out the sunscreen and held it out. "Would you mind?"

This was Kevin, my best friend, yet heat flushed my cheeks. I grabbed the bottle with shaky hands in anticipation of touching his smooth, soft skin.

How was I supposed to touch him? My hands moved up and down his back, sending heat over every part of me. My arms broke out in goosebumps once I made my way down to his lower back. Freckles lined his shoulder blades and the top of his back. His smooth skin felt so good beneath my fingers. I hated for this moment to come to an end.

A dark shadow passed over me while I finished putting the last bit of sunscreen on his neck. My smile faded as I looked up at a thin, beautiful woman standing in front of us.

"Hi, Kevin."

He got to his feet. "Tracey, hello. What are you doing over here?"

"My family is renting a cabin on Pine Beach for the weekend. I was just going to text you and then I saw you were here as if it was meant to be."

Her voice was deep, much deeper than I expected coming

from her tiny body. Her hair was shoulder length and brown, but her highlights were so thick it made her look like more of a blonde. Although the dark roots gave her away.

She did not look at me once or acknowledge my presence while she spoke with Kevin. She was into him and not happy he was here with another woman. Was I invisible?

"Tracey, meet my best friend, Lindsey. She lives here on the lake."

Finally.

She clenched her teeth as she nodded my way. "Hi," she said, with a pinched expression.

"Hi."

I laid down to avoid her awkward stare. At least she was finally looking at me, I guess.

"Tracey and I both go to Duluth East. We sat next to each other in calculus last semester." He acted as though everything was fine. He had missed the body language and friction between us.

Tracey stuck out her chest and pushed her hair behind her shoulders. "I never would have made it through that class without you." She grabbed onto his forearm with a squeeze.

Kevin was buying right into it. He smiled at her.

"I'm going to the bathroom," I said, and I walked away.

I did not want to see his reaction, nor did I care to see hers. I hoped she was gone by the time I came back.

I walked back to the blanket, and she was laying in my spot on her back, one leg bent as if trying so show off her legs. Kevin was sitting, staring out into the water with a football in his hand.

He caught the anger in my eyes and stood up to meet me. "Want to play catch with me?"

Anything to get away from the blonde bimbo. I was certain she would follow us, but she just laid there on the blanket, pulling down her dark shades every time a good-looking guy passed by.

I followed Kevin up the hill to the only place not crowded with people.

He tossed me the football, and I dropped it.

"I've never thrown a football before."

He came up behind me and positioned my fingers in between the laces. He put his hand on mine and pulled it back over my shoulder, extending my elbow. My heart fluttered beneath his touch. He jogged back to where he started, hands out in front of him, ready to catch the ball. I threw it almost perfect. It spiraled toward him, and he raised an eyebrow my way.

Playing catch was a little awkward at first, but I figured out how to throw it pretty fast. I had a good teacher.

"You have a good arm," he said, and threw it back.

"Thanks."

"I'm sorry about Tracey. She's really not that bad."

I laughed. "Are you kidding? She has the biggest crush on you. It's obvious."

He blushed as he caught the ball I threw. He tossed it back and forth between his hands. "I'm not into her like that. I'm horrible at turning people down, and she's just a friend, anyway."

"How come?"

"I don't know. I just feel bad."

I laughed. "Sounds like a good problem to have. Better than not getting any attention at all."

I felt my face grow hot. He knew I was talking about myself. That is what sucks about having a crush on my best friend. He knows me all too well.

He walked toward me, and together we walked down the path in the woods toward the campsites.

"The truth is, I have my eyes on only one woman and she is the one that does not seem to look at me in that way."

He put his hand around my waist, and I put mine around his back as we walked. He cradled the football in his other hand. "How about we get some ice cream?"

I nodded. Who was this mystery girl who was dumb enough not to want him back? I was jealous of all the women in his life I'd never met. I hated that he had another life I was not a part of. He was my best friend, and I needed to stop swooning over him all the time. I was making myself crazy.

We ordered our usual and knocked them together as we sat down on the bench outside the CC gas station. The beautiful RV park for permanent campers was a lot like Pine Beach, but the resorts were unique in their own ways and different.

He took a big bite of his cone and then put his finger in mine.

"Why do you always have to do that?"

"Because I know it bothers you and it's fun."

His leg touched mine, but he did not pull it away. My heart fluttered. If he kept this up, my heart would explode.

"Lyndsey, I've never met anyone like you. I never expected a girl would end up being my best friend. I feel like we've known each other forever."

The friend zone, great.

"There's nothing I can't tell you. I've never felt so connected to someone in my life."

I was not sure what to say to that, so I said an awkward, "Thanks."

"I'm serious. I think I'm ..." His voice trailed off, but our faces were closing in like magnets.

We were so close I felt the coolness of his breath, and smelled the sweetness of the gum in his mouth he stole from my bubble gum ice cream. I pulled away and jumped to my feet.

"What's wrong?"

"Nothing. We're friends and once you kiss me, our friendship will never be the same. You're such a hormonal boy sometimes."

The ice cream in my cone slipped out and now his shorts were covered in ice cream and squares of gum.

I dabbed at his leg with my napkin. "I'm sorry."

"I'm sorry, I guess I wasn't thinking. I won't do it again, okay?"

"Race you to the lake," I said, to relieve the awkwardness. We ditched what was left of our cones in the garbage and took off running. My flip-flops weren't the best for running, and I tripped over my own feet. He turned back to look at me and dropped his football. I stopped and watched him try to catch it. My stomach hurt from laughing so hard when it bounced out of his reach and rolled into the sand by the lake.

He turned back and smiled at me. "We're a hot mess today, aren't we? He ran down the hill, past his football, and dived into the water. I walked down the hill, and I was just about to put my foot in the water when I saw a shadow to my right.

Kevin surfaced, and his head turned when he saw Tracey running toward him. I stopped and watched as she splashed him, and he grabbed her around the waist and threw her deeper into the lake. They were both laughing and splashing each other. He glanced at me for just a moment before she splashed him again, stealing back his attention. He splashed her back and forgot I was there.

"I'm going for something to eat," I said, but it was hard for him to hear me over their stupid, happy flirting. I went back to my picnic blanket and ate the cookies I planned on giving to Kevin. They were supposed to be a surprise but I needed them more than he did.

He would never pick me over a girl like Tracey. Plus, I lived over an hour and a half away from him most of the year. I did not want to stop being best friends with him but it hurt so much to see him flirting with her. Every day I spent with him made me fall more and more in love with him. Maybe not letting him kiss me was a good thing. If we were to date, I would lose him one day as my best friend and that I could not take. He was my other half.

*Now*

I chose my one-sleeve purple silk top and long skirt with a slit down the side to wear to the wedding. Although my shoulder length hair would not cover my naked shoulder, the shirt was elegant and more beautiful than sexy. My diamond necklace with a small gold chain and small pearl, hung off my collarbone and gave me an even more elegant appearance.

My nude-colored Spanx sucked in my midsection. I was uncomfortable already, unable to take deep breaths, but I looked good and felt even better.

I pulled out my beach waver, unsure of the outcome with my short hair, but it ended up looking better than expected. I replaced my black-rimmed glasses with contacts and slipped matching pearls in my ears. I found the perfect shade of purple lipstick to match my silk top.

I was ready to go.

I walked over to Maddy and Brad's house in my slippers, my heels in my hand.

The door opened as I approached, and Maddy stood there looking stunning in her blue dress with a high neckline.

"You look gorgeous," she said and pulled me in for a hug.

"I don't remember the last time I saw you with contacts." She winked at me. "Eat your heart out Kevin Finney."

I laughed. "This isn't for him. I put a little extra effort into my appearance when I'm nervous." It was only partly for him.

She pulled David out of the highchair and put him on her hip. "Sure."

"Hello, sweet boy," I said lightly pinching his sweet cheeks.

"You look beautiful, too, by the way. I love your dress."

"I actually feel like a person again. It's hard with small babies." She rubbed noses with David. "Isn't it, sweetheart? But you're worth it."

Maddie's lip quivered and I knew she was thinking about Ariel.

"Where's my brother? Is he trying to be fashionably late?"

Maddy wiped away a tear under her eye, but I avoided addressing her sadness because it would only make her cry harder. She no longer tried to ignore the pain, but let it be a part of her without shame.

Brad walked into the kitchen in a suit and tie.

"Your tie is all screwed up. Here, let me help," Maddy said. She handed David to me and redid Brad's tie. I kissed his cheeks and watched the cute couple. Brad gazed at Maddy with so much love and lust in his eyes. I turned away because I did not want to see my brother taking off her clothes with his eyes. It was just too weird. But the love in his eyes stayed with me. I wanted someone to look at me that way, and time was running out as the years kept speeding by.


The outdoor ceremony happened beside the Finneys cabin on top of the hill. The yard where I'd spent hot summer days playing bocce ball and croquet with Kevin and our brothers, and where we had Finney family picnics did not seem the same. A large white tent with tables and chairs was wrapped in pink and white bows, and strings of lights hung from the roof of the enormous tent. It was elegant and beautifully lit for when nightfall blanketed the beach.

Centerpieces of different hues of pink roses lit up the tables, and a chiffon runner decorated the head table.

A violinist and pianist began playing, and my brother escorted my family to the groom's side. Brad had received a frantic call from Troy just a week ago. His usher was unable to make it to the wedding, due to deployment, and he asked Brad to fill in. Brad and Troy were best friends back in the day, but Troy had a big family and they had lost touch over the years, so Brad had no hard feelings. He was honored to fill in, even if it was more out of convenience.

The seats filled up rather quickly, and everyone gazed at the water as the groom came riding in on a boat. The driver was a cousin of the Finney's. He pulled up alongside the dock and Troy got out and walked up the hill. Just as he reached the arbor, beautifully decorated in pink roses and lace tied into bows, an engine roared. Three bridesmaids rode up on the back of jet skis with men in no shirts but bow ties driving. The guys got off first and helped the women onto the dock. Their short pink dresses hung loosely, their white swimsuits peaking from underneath. Pink roses were bobby pinned in their hair.

They had huge smiles on their faces as they stepped off the jet skis in their flip-flops.

Everyone stood and applauded them. The men were given button up white shirts to put on, and they pulled the ties down over their collars. I recognized Ethan on the same boat as Kevin. They stepped out of the boat, but I could not take my eyes off Kevin long enough to look at Ethan. The muscles on his chest were bulging and his stomach was defined. I felt a bit warm, but turning my head away was not an option. Even when he put his shirt on and buttoned it halfway up, he still looked as handsome as I'd imagined. I had no idea he had a body like that underneath his stuffy uniform, but I guess he had to stay in shape to be a police officer.

The beautiful bride rode in on the front of a wakeboard boat. She was standing on a cushion, her arm entwined in her father's. The boat slowly cruised to the dock. I was sure Victoria gave strict instructions not to go too fast or her hair would be a mess by the time she reached shore.

Troy's face lit up as his bride slowly walked up the stairs toward him. His eyes sparkled at the sight of her. He wiped his brow and kept smiling.

As the wedding party made their way up the aisle, I stared at Kevin again. He scrunched his eyes together when he saw me, and flashed me a smile.

To say the wedding was brilliant would be an understatement. The ceremony was sexy and elegant, and a wedding I'd never forget. As they said their vows and Troy took Victoria in her arms, I held my breath.

They held hands and walked down the aisle, as we all stood to cheer for the new married couple. Kevin locked arms with the bridesmaid, and his eyes met mine. I looked away. I did not want him to see me caring enough to look at him.

The wedding party disappeared once they walked past everyone, and I was pretty sure they were stealing the bride and groom and going bar hopping at Riverside and Bimbo's restaurants, or even the Viking Bar and Grill, before the reception began.

We were all seated at the tables when the wedding party returned and were introduced. They all had on aviator sunglasses and danced their way to their tables. Kevin came out with a beautiful blonde bridesmaid and gave her a twirl and a dip, and I caught a glimpse of the old Kevin before the seriousness of police work consumed him, and daily life dealing with the general public on their worst days dragged him down.

The dinner was full of silverware tinkling against wine glasses and lots of kissing. Troy had found his person. His eyes glistened during that first kiss, and they were swept away as if they were the only two people in the room. I felt a little like a third wheel sitting next to Brad and Maddy until my mom and aunt showed up. They stayed for dinner and then mom said she was just too tired to stay any longer and they went back to town.

The music started up and the newlyweds hit the dance floor. All eyes were on them and it was so beautiful I had to excuse myself to use the bathroom. I was going to ruin my makeup with all the crying.

The father-daughter song ended, and so did my third glass of pinot. I made my way to the bar to distract myself from keeping an eye on where Kevin was all night.

"Two Colorado Bulldogs."

I shivered at Kevin's voice behind me.

"Maybe I was going to get another glass of wine," I said. I turned my head. His face was close to mine. I stared at his lips. They were beautiful lips. How many lips touched those lips since I last locked lips with him?

His smile deflated. "You could never resist a good bulldog. How did you know I was ordering it for you?" His gaze slid to my mouth. Were you?"

"Well, yeah." He paused and took a drink. "Do you know what I think?"

I shook my head because I could not get a word out if I tried right now.

"I think we know each other way too well and that's why you're ready to take those shoes off and dance with me, like we used to."

I thanked the bartender and took a sip. The sweetness of the cream like candy on my tongue. I loved making him wait.

I set down my drink on the table and he followed me. I kicked off my shoes before he took my hand in his and led me onto the dance floor. He placed both of my hands behind his neck and put his arms around my waist, gradually pulling me into him.

"Remember those days at the Old Howard, back when it was run like a club? We used to dance for hours," he said, his mouth close to my ear.

Kevin's breath on my ear made my arms break out in goosebumps. "You were one hell of a bar back. I never ran out of beer when I was bartending when you were there. That was a long time ago, back in the old college days."

"We were quite a team, weren't we? It's well known you were the best tipper of all the wait staff," Kevin said while pulling me even closer to him.

I looked into his eyes. The light lines beginning to form like crow's feet made him even sexier, because it showed he'd lived. It also reminded me that we let too many years go by not talking to each other.

"Do you remember how we'd sneak out and dance after our shift, even though we weren't twenty-one yet? Craig would get so mad, but he never did kick us out."

He laughed at the memory. "That's because we never tried to drink. That's what having two law enforcement cadets as bar staff does for you. He knew if we drank our school life would be over."

With a tilt of my head, I smiled up at him. "What about those guys in our first year who stole the beer truck?"

He threw his head back and laughed at the memory. "They were so stupid. They lost everything. And to find out the truck was empty, not a bottle of beer in it. Can you imagine?"

"They got kicked out of the program for nothing, but at least they didn't kill anyone."

"That's the thing," he said, as he dipped me back without warning. .

I let myself fall back in his arms because I knew he would never drop me. After all these years he still had my trust.

"A few bad cadets or cops make all of us look so bad."

So true. "Police are never recognized for saving lives and stopping drunk drivers and drugs from coming into the area or running into dangerous situations when the rest of us are running out."

"Ah, if only everyone thought like you," he said, his face so close to mine it would only take a couple inches to put my lips on his. "I'm so sorry again for—"

I placed a finger over his lips, and he turned silent.

"Don't say sorry again, okay? You didn't know. I put myself in that position. It's my job. Let's talk about something else."

I twirled myself in his hand and came back into his arms, our noses almost touching.

"What do you want to know about me, Lyndsey Jones?"

"Why did you and Tracey get divorced?" Anything but that. Why did I say that? My heart pounded as I waited for his response. There was no way to take it back now. My spanx suddenly felt too tight, my lungs unable to breathe in air.

He cleared his throat, not expecting such a blunt question so fast, I'm sure. "Well, Tracey and I settled. We weren't really in love. I wanted to have kids and she didn't. It just wasn't meant to be, I guess."

"I'm sorry."

He shrugged. "It is what it is."

He wanted to have kids? Why was I so excited at the thought? I didn't want kids, did I?

The song ended and we both grabbed our drinks off the table. He took my hand and walked beside me.

"Take a walk down to the lake with me."

More of a command than a question, but I followed without a word. Maybe it was the alcohol getting to me or maybe it was just Kevin Finney, but there was nothing I wanted more than to be alone with him in our old stomping grounds.

Instead of sitting on the Finney's dock, he led me to my parents' dock and took off his socks and shoes and put his feet in the water. I followed his lead.

The cold water cooled down my body temperature. A slight wind blew, so the mosquitoes were not carrying us away.

"Can I ask you a question?" He did not look at me. I stiffened. The question would be heavy. "What's that?"

"Why did you choose social work?"

"Because I didn't want any other kid to go through what you went through with your dad and not feeling safe. I thought I could stop it from happening to someone else, but I didn't realize how difficult it would be."

I looked over at him. His mouth was open, his eyes wide.

"I hated how much he hurt you."

He reached over and pushed hair out of my eyes. Our eyes met for a little too long, and I turned away.

He grabbed my chin, and gave me no choice but to stare into his eyes.

"That is the sweetest thing anyone has ever said to me."

"Yeah, well, I also wanted to be a cop."

"Why did you go to law enforcement school?"

I took a couple gulps of my drink to stall or be brave enough to answer his question.

"To make my father proud, I guess. I had to give it a try and see if it was for me. After ... you know ... well, I guess I wanted to run away from anything law enforcement related. Anyway, I always had social work in the back of my mind."

"After what?" He frowned as if he did not know what I was talking about. But I would not spell it out for him. I wanted to forget. If he didn't already know, I would not be the one to tell him.

I stared at him, waiting to see some recognition in his expression. "After what happened at your apartment that night. You know ... after the party?"

We both jumped at a flash of light and the bang of fireworks. Just like the Finneys to go above and beyond with fireworks and the whole works.

We stood and watched their beauty reflecting off the lake.

He put his arm around me and lifted my chin as he pulled me toward him. Just as our lips finally touched, Tracey's annoying, deep voice interrupted us.

"There you are, Kev. I've been looking everywhere for you."

Of course, Tracey was here. Of course.

# Then

I glanced up at them as Kevin and Tracey made their way to shore. They trudged through the shallow water and toward my picnic blanket. Tracey was running her fingers through her hair. She stopped to playfully shove Kevin, but he caught himself, and she said something too low for me to hear. He smiled, so I knew the feelings were mutual. They were definitely flirting, despite Kevin's empty words from earlier.

The minute they reached my blanket, Tracey put her sandy feet on my towel. I had to get away. I stood up and took off my t-shirt. I acted like I did not notice Kevin staring at me in my suit. I walked away from them and toward the water.

"Where are you going?" Kevin said, as if he was innocent, and the last half hour never happened. Maybe he did not think I could see or hear him out there? Who couldn't hear their playful banter? They were annoyingly loud.

I kept walking without turning back. "I'm going for a swim." My voice came out angry, and he would have to be an idiot not to know I was pissed off. I could care less. I just wanted her to go away.

I half expected him to call out my name and run after me,

but he didn't. I focused on the sound of boat motors and children's laughter in the distance to distract myself.

I walked out quite a way because McCarthy Beach was pretty shallow. As a child, I'd be so far out from shore, and the water would only be chest deep. My mom was always afraid we would drown, and our screams would be silenced by the distance between us. Right now I was okay with it because I could go far out and not hear their giggles and flirty voices. Kevin may be a man, but I never realized how a pair of boobs and a tiny swimsuit could change him so much.

I dove under.. As I swam under the water, my body relaxed and for just a moment, I did not think about him or them. When I came up for air, I heard a splash and turned around. There stood Kevin with a pouty lip and his hands extended as if asking for a hug.

"I'm sorry for being a jerk, Lyndsey Jones. Forgive me?"

I smirked and shook my head. He knew it was hard for me to stay mad at him. I checked the shore for Tracey, but it was hard to see that far away. I blocked the sun with my hand, and tried to see her on shore. "Where did she go?"

"I asked her to leave so I could swim with my best friend."

That was an easy way to wipe the smirk off my face. Friend zoned again. I did not understand men. He was sending so many mixed signals, which left me even more confused. But why was I worrying about it? I needed to appreciate this moment here and now, alone with him.

I splashed him before diving under the water and swimming as far as I could. When I could no longer breathe, I poked my head out. His back was to me, but he turned around just before I dove under again. Opening my eyes, I spotted his legs and tried to trip him, but he grabbed me and pulled me up.

"The water isn't that clear," he said. Then he dunked me while I held onto his neck.

I came up to the sounds of, "Kevin, Kevin."

Tracey was riding on a girl's shoulders. She just could not take a hint.

Kevin stared at them. "What are you ladies doing?"

"We thought you guys might want to have a chicken fight."

Kevin looked at me curiously, and when I didn't answer, he said, "Nah. We're about ready to go in."

"Oh, come on. Your friend seems a bit boring. It's just one little chicken fight. You aren't afraid, Lyndsey, is it?'

I looked back at him. "Let's just do one round and we can go."

"You sure?"

I nodded. He dove underneath me and through my legs. I let out a scream of surprise, and leaned forward to keep my balance once he stood up. I laughed at how stupid I felt right then.

Kevin moved us closer to Tracey and her friend. I steadied myself with my hands on his head until we were within arm's length. Tracey smirked at me and as we entwined our fingers, she dug her nails into my hands.

I screamed out, "What the hell?"

"Oh, I'm sorry, I didn't realize you were so weak."

I quickly taught myself how to attack her without losing my balance. I pushed her with the force of my anger, and she pushed back. We grabbed hands again, and I squeezed her fingers as hard as I could. She tried to grab both of my hands with her one hand, with no success. I was stronger than I looked, but then again so was she.

"Look, Brad Pitt!"

Against the odds, she fell for it and turned her head. I threw her off balance, along with the girl underneath her when she turned around. They both fell backward into the water. Kevin dove under and let me off his shoulders.

We both laughed.

"Quick thinking," he said with a high five.

Tracey let out a sigh. "One more?"

"No, I think we better go now, but that was so much fun. We should do it again soon." My sarcasm was obvious. She splashed me as we walked away.

Beating her was so satisfying. Now she knew better than to pick a fight with me.

"Call me later, Kev. Maybe we can hang out tomorrow," Tracey said.

He nodded, but I think he heard the sound of desperation in her voice. She may be pretty and skinny, but she was a snob. She'd probably move onto the next guy as soon as she got what she wanted from Kevin. It was all a game to her. I knew girls like her.

"Well, that was fun," I said, my voice dripping with sarcasm.

"Sure was."


We were sitting in my parents' boat, tied to the dock, and waiting for Brad so we could do some skiing and wakeboarding. My brother was on the phone with one of his girlfriends, and didn't seem in a hurry to get off the phone any time soon. Which girlfriend was it this week? I lost track. He was a ladies' man, and had a line of them in waiting. He was cocky and, for some reason women liked that.

"It's weird to think you have a whole other life in Duluth when you're not here."

He smiled with half his face, the sexy way that made my heart flutter. My cheeks grew warm. I checked if he noticed, but he showed no sign.

"I feel the same about you. Tell me about Hibbing High School."

I stared at my hand. "It's just a normal high school. I have a couple good friends, but it's not the same without Kat there.'

"Do you have a boyfriend?"

This definitely got my attention. Did he care? Would he be jealous?

"Nope. Why, do you have a girlfriend?"

"I did, but we broke up."

This was my chance.

"What about Tracey? She seems to be very into you."

He ran his fingers through his perfect hair. "I told you, she's not my type. Don't get me wrong, she's beautiful."

I wanted to gag. Instead, I half stuck my fingers down my throat and let out a gag for dramatic effect.

He threw his shirt at me. "Cute."

I shrugged.

"The problem is, she knows she's beautiful. Unlike you. You're perfect, everyone can see that, but you're too humble to ever believe it."

"Stop, you're embarrassing me. I'm pretty sure my brother inherited all the cockiness in this family and I was left with lack thereof. Will he ever get off the phone? Sometimes I want to get him back for being such a jerk to me."

He shot me a devilish look. "And he's a jerk to these women that line up for him. You still want to get your brother back? Teach him a little lesson he won't forget?"

I turned around to make sure Brad was nowhere near us.

" I like this side of you. What do you have in mind?"

"Your brother is always the first to take a shower as soon as we're done boating, right?"

Where was he going with this. "Yes?"

"Your parents are gone, right?"

"My dad is working, and my mom is in town getting groceries."

"Follow me," he said, as he slung his backpack over his shoulder and headed for my house. Brad was still on the phone. We snuck right past him into the house.

Kevin turned around right before the bathroom door and pulled a bottle out of his bag. "So, you know how your brother loves the shampoo that smells like pine trees?"

"Yeah." Were we getting back at him by giving him another bottle?

"No one else uses that shampoo, right?"

I nodded and crossed my arms. "Where are you going with this exactly?"

He peeked behind me to make sure no one was around.

"I bought a bottle of his shampoo and squirted most of it out except a little in the bottom, and mixed it with bright red hair dye."

My heart raced. What a great idea. I grabbed the bottle out of his hand. "No way! You're a genius."

"I know," he said, with a sexy smirk. "Grab his bottle in the shower and replace it with this one. He'll take a shower and when he gets out, he'll look like an eraser."

"I love it! You know how important his looks are to him. He has a date tonight, it's perfect!"

I rushed into the shower, switched out the bottle. Kevin took the bottle and gave me a high five.

We climbed into the boat and tried not to smirk about what was yet to come.

"Who's ready to ski?"

The sound of my brother's voice had us both close to tears. We tried to stop laughing, but once we started we could not stop.

Kevin smiled at me and then put on his sunglasses, and looked away to keep a straight face.

Brad took us on Little Sturgeon where the boat traffic was

light and the water had fewer waves, which was great for skiing.

As soon as Brad turned the boat off, I jumped to the back of the boat and put on my life jacket. Brad threw out the rope. I sat on the boat's back deck and put on my trick skis.

The sun was hidden behind some clouds, but the temperature was still about eighty-two degrees outside. The water was warm until I jumped in. It only felt cold for a second, and then it was surprisingly refreshing. As I leaned into the water, my skis in the air, and the rope held between my legs, I signaled Kevin with a nod that I was ready to go. He pulled down his sunglasses and winked at me, then said something to my brother.

This small gesture took my breath away, and as Brad hit the gas, my arms were not extended, and the rope slipped right through my fingers. He circled the boat around and Kevin hung his head over the side of the boat. This was not normal for me. I'd done this so many times.

"What happened, Lyndsey?"

"Really?" I laughed and focused on the rope, and not the warm feeling breaking out on my cheeks. He did that on purpose.

Once the rope was tight, I nodded again, and Brad hit the gas. I pulled right up and focused on keeping my knees and feet close together. Trick skis felt more slippery than regular skis in the water. I slalomed and Kevin watched me closely as I edged back and forth inside the wakes. This was the first time he saw me ski.

After a few minutes, I jumped the wake, clearing the water and landed in the center of the wake with perfect balance. I crossed back over, and when I jumped this time, I was thrown off balance and let go of the rope. But I was just warming up. I would hit it just right on the next try. I was getting into my groove.

On the next run, I showed the boys up by doing a front-to-back surface turn, pausing, then doing a back to front surface turn. Kevin hooted and clapped, cheering me on.

Once my arms were like rubber and all my grip strength was gone, I crawled into the boat, which was quite a struggle with weak and sore arms. Kevin leaned over the back of the boat and pulled me up. He stared into my eyes before he pulled me into the boat.

Once I was back in the boat, Kevin strapped on Brad's wakeboard. Inexperienced, he fell many times. This was the first time I got to see him. We'd gone out a few times, but we only tubed, and knee boarded.

Brad jumped in the water on his wakeboard while talking some smack to Kevin and saying, "Watch and learn."

I took over driving while he showed Kevin up by doing side flips off the wake. Kevin was obviously impressed by his cheers with each trick Brad landed.

We were worn out before the sun even went down. Brad pulled the ropes in and rolled them up while Kevin and I put the wakeboard away and sat at the back of the boat. Brad made another phone call to his date for tonight. Of course, this reminded Kevin and me of what was to come, and we giggled in the back of the boat.

"You looked really good out there," Kevin said, once we stopped laughing. "I guess it's not just shooting you're a pro at."

I jumped in surprise when he put his hand on my thigh.

"You scared me," I said. My cheeks burned. "Thank you. You did pretty good yourself."

"I suck. I've never seen a girl ski like that in person before. Where did you learn to do those tricks?"

I shrugged, trying not to focus on the feel of his hand on

my bare leg. "We grew up on a lake. Both of my parents' trick ski, and they taught me. I may suck at most sports, but growing up on a lake you tend to ski a lot. I've had a lot of practice over the years."

"So, you've never competed or anything?"

"No. It's just for fun. I never wanted to. I enjoy being here on the chain with no pressure, doing what I love with my family and friends."

"It must be nice to be so close to your family. I wish my parents cared as much as yours do."

I put my hand on top of his. "You're always welcome to ski with us. Your parents are doctors, I'm sure it isn't easy for them to get away from their jobs."

He forced a smile and gazed at the sky as the sun began to set. The clouds were blocking what was left of the sun, and the rays spread through the sky like spotlights. The mirrored reflection off the water brought solace to my soul, and made this moment with him perfect. I didn't want it to end. I loved the water, the sun, Side Lake, and everything there was to do in the water. When I met Kevin I realized the lake is truly who I am. It just took sixteen or so years to figure it out.

"My family has more money than we know what to do with, but I'd give it all up for time with them, you know?"

"I'm sure it isn't easy. You and Troy are close though?"

"Yeah, he's my brother, but I wish my parents were around. It's different. My brother and I are pretty close most days, and I know he has my back no matter what, even when we hate each other. I just wish my parents were there for me once in a while. I know I'm almost an adult, but I want them to take my temperature when I'm sick, make me chicken noodle soup, take me for a boat ride, eat s'mores with me out by the fire at night. I never got any of that." He looked down in his lap. "I want the kind of love you have. I must sound so stupid."

"It's not all sunshine and roses in my world either."

We stared at each other in silence until he leaned in to kiss me, this time I did not stop him. Before our lips could touch, the sound of my brother's voice made us both jump.

"Don't tell me the two of you are a thing now. Gross. Does mom know?"

"Shut up," I said. I jumped to my feet. "We aren't a thing."

Brad turned up the radio and I could no longer hear my own thoughts the music was so loud. I was grateful for the distraction and I'm pretty sure Kevin was, too.

"I'm going for a shower," Brad said.

I had almost forgotten what was about to happen.

*Now*

Kevin stood up. "Hey Tracey. When did you get here?"

"Just a few minutes ago. I would have been here earlier, but I had some car problems."

She did not glance my way.

"I was hoping you would say hello to your brother with me. With everything that happened with us, I'm a little nervous to show up in there on my own."

"Don't be nervous. It's Troy and Victoria."

She held out her hand and he took the bait, putting his hand in hers. He turned to look at me as if he just remembered I was there.

"Want to come inside?"

I nodded. "I'll be in there in a minute. Go ahead without me. I'll be right behind you."

He stared at me for a moment, as if debating whether or not I'd run away.

I forced a smile. "Seriously. I just need a minute."

"Okay," he said.

This was what Tracey always did. She had a way of getting people to do whatever she wanted. She was pushy and always in control. Even at work she would speak out in meetings, stomping over everyone else's opinions. If that wasn't bad enough, everyone would agree with her because they did not want to be her next victim.

I tried not to watch as Tracey and Kevin chatted with Troy across the room. Kevin and Troy both took their suit coats off and placed them over chairs at the table. Standing in their vests, drinks in hand, they laughed and turned their heads to watch the beautiful bride make her way toward them.

Tracey hugged Victoria, and as the four of them chatted, she placed her head on Kevin's shoulder and put her arm around him. She was tiny, maybe five foot one, and he was close to six foot two.

I held my breath, my body growing warm and stiff. Why did this hurt so much? This was what jealousy looked like. I turned around to find Ethan standing behind me.

"Lyndsey Jones?" He looked me up and down and extended his arms with a grin. "You haven't changed a bit. You're every bit as beautiful as when we were teenagers."

"Ethan?" I placed my drink on the table next to me and hugged him. He smelled amazing, like soap and pine needles.

We pulled away, and I could not wipe the smile off my face. He looked amazing. Even more gorgeous than the last time I saw him. He no longer had that little boy face. He would turn any woman's head. Wait until I told Kat. She would never believe this.

In today's world, we knew how most people were doing by following them on social media. Well, we saw what everyone wanted us to see, anyway. Both Ethan and Kevin were nowhere to be found online. Along with most of the Finneys. They kept their personal lives off-line.

Ethan looked behind me. "Is Kat here, too?"

"No, I still can't get her to come back to Side Lake after all these years."

"Is it because of her mom? Is her mom still crazy?"

I laughed, remembering that day in the gazebo way too well. "I don't know. She lives alone. She's a bit of a loner. Other than seeing her friends down at Riverside or tanning by the beach on her lawn chair when I've boated by, I don't see her, let alone talk to her."

He shook his head and took another drink out of his clear plastic glass.

I looked back at the foursome in the corner. Kevin and Tracey seemed cozier than before.

I turned back to him. "You want to dance?"

"You know what? I'd love to." He put his glass down on the table next to mine and took my hand to lead me into the middle of the dance floor. The fairy lights lit up the linoleum dance floor, along with a spotlight. Ms. Finney had gone all out for her oldest son's special day. I wasn't surprised. She was one of the best oncologists at the Mayo Clinic in Rochester. I knew because that's all I found out about the Finney's.

We had so much fun dancing to *Staying Alive* by The Bee Gees. My pointer fingers got quite the workout. Ethan and I laughed and danced around each other, and I forgot about Kevin and Tracey for a time. As the song ended, we were both breathless, and I had to wipe the sweat from my forehead with the back of my hand.

*Wonderful Tonight* by Eric Clapton blared through the speakers, and Ethan put out his hand. I took it and he put his hands on my waist, mine clasped behind his neck. There was enough distance between us to fit another person. Enough space so we could talk.

"How is Kat?" His voice came out more of a whisper. The look in his eyes showed sadness.

"She's doing well. She's a child protection social worker in the Cities. She likes it a lot more than I do."

He shot me a questioning look.

"I'm also a CPS worker here."

He nodded. "I see."

"She lives with her boyfriend. They don't have any kids. She stays away because her non-existent relationship with her mom is still too toxic. I try to see her as much as I can."

"I'm glad she's doing well. And that she's happy. Tell her hello for me?"

"I definitely will. So, what are you doing now? Where are you living?"

"New York."

I stopped dancing and shook my head. "That's great, Ethan, really great. New York City, huh?"

"Yeah, but I can work remote so I'm thinking about moving back to Minnesota."

I felt a presence behind me. Ethan's eyes raised. And then his deep voice spoke. "Mind if I cut in?"

Kevin.

"She's all yours, buddy," Ethan said letting go of my waist. "It was so great catching up, Lyndsey. Take care." He took my hand and gave it a light kiss before walking away.

Kevin put his hand on my lower back, instantly sending chills up my back and arms. How did the smallest touch from him make me so giddy with excitement?

"Where's Tracey?"

He let out a grunt. "You still aren't a fan, huh? How on Earth did the two of you end up working together anyway?"

I opened my mouth to answer, but he put his finger on my lips to silence me.

"Don't answer that. I don't want to spend the night talking about her. I want to talk to you."

"Can I ask you a question?"

I nodded. "You do have my full attention, Mr. Finney."

He grinned and dipped me back. Once I was vertical again, he pulled me in. The song was faster, but here we were the only ones still slow dancing.

"Let's go for a walk."

"That wasn't a question."

He smiled and shook his head. "I guess it wasn't, was it?"

"That was."

He smiled.

I led him around his parents' enormous house and into my yard. We made our way down to the dock.

He glanced at my house with the dark windows and no lights. "Your parents still live here?"

"No, my dad is in a nursing home, and my mom lives with her sister. It's been a tough couple of years."

"I'm so sorry. I've missed so much of your life."

I wanted to scream at him for all the pain he caused me over the years, but instead I just smiled and bit my lip. "I try to see them every morning on my way to work, and help out as much as I can. A lot has changed."

"I'm so sorry I never told you about my dad passing away."

I nodded. "I know."

"I kept waiting for you to show up at the funeral."

I raised my eyebrows. "How was I supposed to show up if you didn't tell me?"

"I know. I screwed up, but I kept waiting for you show up that day anyway. I needed you. I guess I just expected you to know."

"You needed me? But you hated me."

He put his hand behind my head. "Let's not talk about that tonight."

We both stared at each other until it got awkward.

"Since no one lives in your house anymore, want to go swimming like in the old days."

"Kevin, we're adults now."

"Exactly," he said, unbuttoning his dress shirt. It dropped to the dock, his eyes still locked with mine. "We can't get in trouble from our parents anymore."

"It's going to be cold," I said. My heartbeat was pounding in my ears and my hands shook.

He unzipped his pants and dropped them on the dock.

He was in the water before I could say anything. I heard the splash and then he dove under.

I walked to the edge of the dock and waited for him to surface. "Cold?"

The lights from my motion detector gave us enough light to see him.

"Refreshing. I think you should come warm me up," he said, holding onto the side of the dock.

"You're drunk and swimming. I think this is a very bad idea, deputy."

He put his hands on the dock and pushed his upper body out of the water, his arms supporting his weight. Every bulge in his arms was engraved in my mind. I could not take my eyes off him. He jumped to his feet at the edge of the dock, and water splashed up at me. I hopped back.

He gave me that look I'd never forget. I was ready for him to throw me in the lake but he changed his mind at the last minute and kissed me instead.

Maybe it was the alcohol, but I surprised myself by not fighting back. He lifted me up, and I wrapped my legs around him. He held me above him.

In slow motion, our bodies became unbalanced, and we tipped over the side of the dock. I rose to the surface coughing while trying to breathe again through my drowned lungs.

"Breathe, Lyndsey, breathe. Are you okay?"

He was holding me in his arms again, patting my back.

"I'm so sorry. I guess I was a bit more unsteady than I expected.

I splashed him after coughing again.

"Are you okay? Do I need to call for an ambulance?"

I splashed him again and he covered his eyes. I splashed him harder.

"You're such a jerk, Kevin Finney."

He grabbed my arms and pulled me in. As our lips touched again, my body was no longer shivering. Instead, I was on fire from head to toe.

I thought about pulling away, but I was too excited to finally be in his arms. He dove under the water to unzip my dress and pull it down. I stepped out of it and when his head popped back up, I wrapped my arms and legs around him.

"You have no idea how many years I dreamed of this moment," he said, fiercely pulling me back to his lips. He nibbled on my lip, and I giggled and bit him back.

I pulled off my bra and underwear, and he followed suit. The water was too dark to really see anything, but we could not keep our hands off each other as we explored everything we had missed these past fifteen years. Our passion was more than I'd ever had with a man. He was so caring and loving, and I melted beneath his touch. A little liquid courage and we were finally finishing what we started all those years ago.

Our lovemaking was perfect, until the next morning when I heard a knock at my door before day light. There stood my brother and sister-in-law, staring at our tangled hair and naked bodies hidden beneath an Afghan with more holes than I was comfortable with. I never should have told them my key code.

Brad turned around as soon as he saw us, and walked out the door, "Just friends, huh?"

Then

We tied the boat to the dock, and Brad ran ahead of us to call his girlfriend. Kevin and I sat down on the dock.

"That was so much fun today," Kevin said.

I jumped up. "Brad's going to shower! We have to go!"

Kevin stood up. "How could we forget? This will be epic."

"He's going to scream. I can't wait to see his face."

We raced up the yard. I slid open the door and did a double take. There was my dad in his police uniform with bright pink, almost florescent hair. I was so dead.

I stopped so abruptly that Kevin ran into my back.

"Hey—"

He spotted my dad.

I exchanged a horrified look with Kevin because not only was my dad's hair pink, but he was in his uniform getting ready for work.

"I think I forgot to tie the boat up," I said to Kevin, ready to run.

My dad glanced out the sliding glass door. "It looks tied up to me."

135

"I forgot a buoy." I kept walking. Kevin passed me. We were so dead.

When our feet hit the dock, we both started breathing and laughing.

"I'm pretty sure your dad doesn't look in the mirror very often," Kevin said. "That or he likes his pink hair."

"I can't believe he used my brother's shampoo. He's going to be so mad when he finds out what we did."

"When do you think that will be?"

"Probably when he sees my brother or when he gets to work. His hands had to be pink. How did he not know?"

"I don't think it would turn his hands pink," Kevin said. "I mean probably just slightly. I didn't notice. Did you?"

I shook my head. Any minute now my dad would scream out that door, but the longer we stayed outside, the more I wondered if he'd already left. I hoped he was long gone before he found out.

The clouds were dark and circling us in the sky. The wind picked up and rain was coming.

Kevin opened his mouth to speak, but the sudden downpour took his words away.

He started laughing. I looked around to see if my dad was inside, but it was hard to tell.

"Why are you laughing?"

He laughed louder, harder, unable to sit up now. The rain ran down my face and into my eyes, but all I could do was stare at him. I loved his laugh, and the vein in the middle of his forehead that stuck out when he laughed or yelled or got really frustrated.

I gave him a push and he pushed me back, laughing. It became more of game because neither of us wanted to go inside and chance seeing my father. Instead, we walked to the edge of the dock and put our hands out to feel the water. Kevin opened up his mouth to drink it in.

The rain was surprisingly warm as it soaked our clothes. Once Kevin looked like he was no longer on guard, I pushed him off the dock and into the water. I turned my back and made my way up to the house, still debating whether I should go inside.

"You can't just push me in and walk away, Jonesy."

His voice was muffled as the rain hit the water and ground with such force.

I turned around. "Jonesey?"

"Yeah, Jonesey. It has a good ring to it, right?"

In one swift movement he jumped on the dock and jogged to my side.

The rain turned to hail and stung when it bounced off my body. I used my hand to shield my face.

Kevin pointed to the upside-down canoe. "Over there!"

I followed him, even though I had to go into my house at some point, and it was not much farther than the canoe. The confident way Kevin took charge had me following without thinking twice.

Kevin wrapped his arms around me to keep me warm once we were both under the canoe. His clothes were sopping wet from the lake and the rain. "Do you realize this may be our last summer together, hanging out at the lake?"

He wasn't coming back next summer? What would I do without him? I could not lose both of my best friends.

"Where will you be next summer?"

"I'm hoping to get a security job to build up my resume before I become a cop."

"But won't you stay at your cabin when you aren't working?"

"Maybe, I'm not sure. My parents aren't exactly thrilled I'm not going to med school. A police officer is kind of the exact opposite."

"But it's your dream."

He shook his head and peeked out of the canoe to check out the dark sky. "They don't care. My dad is dying. Last night my mom came running into my room freaking out because my dad fell and couldn't get up."

"What happened?"

"I don't know. They don't really talk to me about it. All I know is my mom couldn't pick him up herself, so I had to help him get into bed. I don't think he has much time left."

"I'm so sorry."

He grabbed my hand. "Don't be. He hates me anyway."

This time I leaned closer and closer until our lips met. An electric current jolted through my body and left me warm. He put his hands around the back of my neck and held me steady while we explored each other's mouths. I knew I would regret this later, but right now I wanted to remember this feeling. This moment of my first kiss.

And just like that, the rain stopped and so did our kiss.

He crawled out from under the canoe. I took the hand he offered and stood.

We walked into my house, and my brother stood by the door laughing. "Dad is so pissed at you."

"Is he here?"

"No, he's on his way to work. He said his hair is pink."

"That was supposed to be you with pink hair," I said.

He shook his head. "You need better aim. You're in so much trouble."

He walked away, and I just stood there, shaking with worry. How angry was my father? Surely, he'd understand it was just a joke?

"I think you need to relax in my hot tub," Kevin said. "There's nothing you can do now. I'm sorry I got you in trouble."

"I'll just have to deal with it later. A hot tub sounds great. Race you there."

I ran out of breath before we reached the stairs that led up to his deck, and stopped to catch my breath. The sliding glass door opened above us, and he brought his finger to his lips to silence me.

"Tyler, you need to stop working. Spend some time with the boys. They would like that. You always said you wished you had more time with them."

"Those worthless pieces of shit? I'd rather not. I have one kid that's going to be a pig and another that's a dork with numbers. Neither one of them will be like us. They're failures. They won't live out my legacy. They won't make anything of themselves, and it's all because of your coddling."

"Me?" Mrs. Finney's voice cracked. "I never say anything to you, Tyler, but you need to be there for those boys. You're too hard on them, and you should love them for who they are. Not despise them because they aren't like you."

We heard a loud slap, and something fall. Kevin pulled away from me. I tried to grab him but missed. He flew up the stairs and I heard loud screams followed by a loud thump and then silence. I ran up after him and stopped when I saw Mr. Finney on the floor and Mrs. Finney with a red cheek."

Mr. Finney groaned through clenched teeth. "You're no tough guy."

I almost felt bad for him, but for the first time ever, Mr. Finney did not look a bit intimidating.

Kevin nodded at me with dismissal. I forced a smile, nodded back, and walked down the stairs. That man was a horrible human being, and I could not feel bad for him.

When I walked in the door, my mother gave me a disappointing look. "Lyndsey Jones, I can't believe you dyed your dad's hair pink."

I tried to explain, but she cut me off.

"Next time, make sure you actually get the person you're trying to trick. Improve your aim." Then she grinned.

I was so stunned, I stood there as she dished me up a plate of lasagna.

"Thanks, mom."

As I lay in my bed that night, looking up at the ceiling fan circling above my head, I was grateful Mr. Finney would not be around much longer, so Kevin and his mother could finally live their lives without a fist in their way.

*Now*

I grabbed the nearest pillow, put it over my head, and screamed.

Kevin laughed and took the pillow off my head. He grabbed my glasses off the coffee table and gently placed them on my nose.

"How are you so calm right now?"

He shrugged. "I haven't had my morning coffee yet?"

I jumped to my feet, taking the blanket with me. I looked back for a glimpse of him in the light.

He was still where I left him, on his side, but his hand was now supporting his head. He was staring at me. Our eyes met, and I smiled. His black boxer briefs covered him, barely. Calvin Klein never looked so good. He did not have a six pack, but he hit the gym regularly and took care of his body.

He was perfect and just looking at him made my body quiver with desire. His skin was smooth and tan. His body was strong, like a work of art, and his chest muscles danced around when he saw me staring at them I turned away. My chest tightened as I hid my face from his view.

"It could have been worse."

I frowned at him.

"It was nowhere near as bad as Kat and Ethan."

I laughed. That was not what I expected him to say. I had forgotten about that incident. Okay, I would never forget about that incident, but it happened so long ago.

With my back to him, I dressed. I turned around to find him with his jeans on, and his back bare as he lifted his t-shirt over his head. I marveled at the breadth of his shoulders.

"This was a onetime thing. You don't have any girlfriends or wives I need to know about. Do you?"

He laughed. "No. No one I am currently seeing."

"And Tracey?"

"What about her?"

I had no idea what to say. They had been married and divorced but he still talked to her. He still called her, and went on dates with her. Weren't they getting back together? But it did not matter, we were never doing this again.

"Nothing," I said with a dismissive tone in my voice. "This isn't going to be weird at work, right?"

He moved closer to me, staring into my eyes. He gripped my chin softly, and tilted my head up. I trembled beneath his touch.

"Tell me you aren't thinking about returning to work soon?" His voice was deep and raspy.

I looked down. "I can't stay away from my job too long. Kids could die, and I'm sure my work phone is blowing up."

"Don't rush it."

"If I could afford it, I would probably never go back. But I shouldn't complain to you. Your job is even harder."

"Lyndsey, you know you can't compare the two. You go into the house with a file, and I go in with a gun, taser, baton, flashlight, and backup. I'm trained for danger."

We lacked protection in my job. Unless we knew danger was a possibility, the police did not come with us. Sometimes I went into some sketchy places without backup or anyone even knowing where I was going.

He moved his hands over the back of my neck, then kissed me lightly at first, which turned passionate and deepened within seconds. My heart fluttered, and my lips tingled. The kiss brought me back to the way he kissed me when we were teenagers.

I could never let him get this close again. He broke my heart too many times, and he would never love me the way I'd always loved him. He broke my heart with every kiss, because he never meant anything by it, and this time was no different. I pulled away.

"What's wrong?"

I stood up. "This was a mistake. We never should have—"

"Made love?"

He stood up and I could not look him in the eyes. "Exactly. Please, get your clothes and leave, okay?"

I did not wait for an answer. I went into my bathroom, locked the door, and took the longest shower of my life. I was not getting out until I was sure he was gone.

The last few weeks had been a lot. Running from a client, scared for my life, Kevin saving my life, just having Kevin back in my life in general, and then having the most passionate sex of my life.

I was giddy at the thought of last night. The way he held me, the way he pleased me, the way he looked at me with such admiration and love in his eyes. But we were drunk, maybe not too drunk, but drunk enough to not be as cautious. Our critical thinking was not at its sharpest. That's what it came down to. All the old feelings coming back. He claimed he did not have feelings for Tracey, but I was sure he did. He was only fooling himself. Hadn't he always had feelings for her?

I knew this was a huge mistake, but I would not forget it happened. Our time together was amazing, and I was single. I always imagined what it would be like to make love to him and now I knew. It hurt how much I still loved him. But pushing him away was my only choice.

I spent the day at home by myself. Staring out at the lake. By the end of the day, I came to the conclusion that I needed to return to work. All I did was worry about my clients when I was at home. Wondering if the kids were safe, and if professionals were trying to get ahold of me. I worried no one was checking on my clients, investigating my cases.

Monday morning I arrived a half hour early for work. My supervisor asked that I meet with her before everyone else got there to discuss my return.

"What do you need? What can I do to make this easier for you?"

Her beautiful curls spiraled out by her ears, her ponytail full. She pushed her glasses up the bridge of her nose. She was a beautiful person inside and out. She made returning to work possible. She was my support, and the person who was always there to help me make the toughest decisions for the best interest of the children.

"I want everyone to treat me the same. I'm not broken, and I can still do my job."

She nodded. "Just don't pretend it didn't happen. It did and it could happen again, but you need to be aware and don't go into a place when you feel like something is off. You're lucky that officer was there."

"Yeah. I guess I am."

"We can talk on our way to the conference room before everyone gets here for the morning meeting. Is there anything else you want to chat about before we go in?"

"Actually, there is."

She smiled gently at me.

"I want to continue working Molly's case. Where are the kids?"

She raised an eyebrow. "Do you really think that's a good idea?"

I had thought about this a lot. "Yes. I won't go there alone."

She looked down, deep in thought. "Okay. Promise me that you not only won't go there alone, but you will let me know if you aren't okay. Promise?"

I nodded.

"The kids are both with the dad. Mom is out of jail, pending fourth degree assault charges."

I gasped. "It's nice to know assaulting your social worker is no big deal."

"I'm sorry, but you know she has a minimal criminal history, with just one drug charge pending. She was let out on pre-trial release but paid her bail so she doesn't have to follow any conditions."

"Of course, she did."

"You have to let it go if you want to keep working with her. This makes me nervous. I have a lot riding on the line here if you get upset."

"I'll be okay, I promise. I'm not going to attack her." I was pissed, but I would never get physical. Not unless I was fighting for my life.

She put her hand on my shoulder. "I'm glad you're back."

I told the story about being assaulted by Molly to my unit at the morning meeting. They all sat there listening and then supported me on my decisions. Even Tracey. I don't think she had a choice. If she were to criticize me after everything that happened, my co-workers would have eaten her alive.

I checked on my clients. First, Tammy and Tyler, but I did

not see Molly. Grandma Ida seemed to be doing okay raising the kids for now and Kelly's UA was negative for meth, which made Ida happy. Kelly's house was getting cleaner, and a dumpster stood outside her front door full of junk from her house. She was serious about getting clean and fighting to get her kids back, and I could not be prouder. My first day back was pretty good overall.

I did not see Kevin until about four o'clock. I was getting ready to leave, and he was in the parking lot talking with Tracey. He yelled out to me, but I got in my car and pulled away before he could catch me. He tried calling twice, but I ignored his calls. This was for the best. Hopefully, I would not have to work with him too much. I had no idea what I would say when we did meet. Why was he always talking to Tracey?

I got home to find Maddy in my kitchen, cooking scrambled eggs and bacon. She'd brought over the highchair and David was cooing. I kissed his cheek before saying hello to Maddy, but she did not seem to mind.

"How was your first day back at work?"

I breathed in the breakfast aroma in the air. Nothing beat coming home to the smell of bacon and breakfast for dinner.

"Good. Oh my gosh, this smells absolutely delicious."

"It's a little hot out for bacon, but I thought we could have a little picnic by the lake. Brad is meeting us here. Maybe we'll take the boat out before it gets dark.

Minnesota summers were the best. It did not get dark until nine or ten at night, whereas in December it would be dark by four.

I lifted David out of his highchair, and took him down to the water. I removed our shoes before setting him in the water. He walked as I held his arm. He was still struggling to balance. The sandy bottom felt refreshing on my feet.

The sound of the light waves crashing on shore made me smile. I loved all the sounds of the lake. At one time I wanted nothing more than to move away, but not anymore.

David splashed his free hand in the water. My mind flashed back to the days I took Ariel down here to do the same thing. Bittersweet memories.

Brad surprised me as he ran into the water and lifted David into the air. David's lips parted and a smile spread across his face. His giggles forced me to laugh with him.

I never thought I wanted kids after Ariel died. I was happy for Maddy when she found out she was pregnant with David after everything she had been through, but Ariel's death scarred me for life. I did not want to have a child and worry about keeping him or her alive. If tragedy happened to Brad and Maddy's kid, when they were the best parents I knew, then it could happen to me. I was not as strong as they were. I did not want a boyfriend because I was too afraid they would want kids. My feelings were not something anyone could understand.

I did not need a man or a child to make me happy, anyway. I definitely didn't need Kevin Finney. I had Brad and Maddy and sweet little David. I had everything I needed.

# Then

~~~

I considered myself a girly girl. I liked to play cars with my brother as a child and I loved target shooting since that first day my father took my brother and me to the range. I loved target shooting, clay pigeon shooting, and grouse hunting, but no one would ever call me a tomboy. I have always worn fancy clothes and pastels. My brother would tease me that Easter vomited in my closet. I put on makeup every day before leaving my house, and spent way too much money on moisturizer.

Here I was sick to my stomach in my blue polo shirt, spit shined boots, and ironed black slacks with a perfect crease down the front and back. I was doing it, I made up my mind. My short brown hair was pulled back in a bun, which was not easy since a ponytail was already a difficult challenge without my hair slipping out. Plenty of hairspray, a couple bobby pins, and I must admit, I looked the part. I was going to school to be a cop.

I walked up the stairs and into the classroom.

We were all dressed the same, yet a bunch of law enforcement students with ironed on badges over the chest made my heart sink. I was roughly fifteen minutes early and only two seats were open. Everyone was so early and on time. I scanned the room for Kevin, but he was nowhere to be seen.

I debated social work and law enforcement school, applying for both. Two weeks ago, I decided law enforcement was where my heart was. I would only know for sure if I tried it. Law enforcement was in my blood. I could always finish the four-year social work program if this did not work out for me.

Kevin was the last person to walk in, seconds after eight.

The instructor, Mr. Fletcher, stood at the front of the classroom, his eyes following Kevin as he sat down. Kevin never saw me and had no idea I was there. Everyone was staring at Kevin because the teacher was watching his every move. My stomach fluttered as he rolled up his sleeves and raised his chin. He glared at Kevin in an intimidating way only a police officer or an angry mother was capable of. I inched lower in my desk, waiting for the confrontation to unravel.

Once Kevin sat down, he noticed all eyes on him, and he glanced around until his eyes locked with our teacher. He jumped up at attention, his chin up, and shoulders back. "I'm sorry I'm late, sir."

His chest puffed out like a soldier. I'd never seen him this way. Was the program this pro military?

The instructor took a step in Kevin's direction. "What's your name, cadet?"

I could not breathe. I wished there was some way I could save him, but he was on his own. I was glad he did not know I was there yet. I'm sure this was embarrassing enough.

"Kevin, sir."

"We go by last names here, cadet."

"Finney, sir."

"Well, Finney, do you think your time is more important than the rest of the class?"

"No, sir."

The teacher paced with no expression as he spoke. "Do you think your time is more important than my time?"

"No, sir," Kevin said.

"Because instead of getting started, we are sitting here waiting for you to show up for class. What was so important that you thought you didn't need to be on time?"

"I had a flat tire, sir."

"I see, well, next time you should think about leaving your house a little earlier in case you have car troubles again."

"Sorry, sir."

"Do you know the protocol in my classroom when students are late?"

He shook his head. "No, sir."

Mr. Fletcher grinned and then turned stone cold, crossing his arms. "Get down and give me fifty pushups."

"Yes, sir."

Without hesitation, he dropped to the floor and started doing perfect pushups. His face was as red as an apple. I watched in absolute shock. The way his muscles bulged in his back and beneath the arms of his polo shirt. When did he get so strong? Several months had passed since I'd seen him, but although he was still thin, he was obviously on a very strict workout routine. Could I do fifty pushups? Note to self, never ever be late for class.

Mr. Fletcher looked over our heads as he spoke. "I guess this is a good time to go over the expectations in my classroom. Never be late is the first rule. Followed by be prepared for class, always wear your uniform, and be respectful. If any of you need to talk to a teacher outside of the classroom, come to our office located right next to the couches in the hallway. You knock on the door and announce your name, proceeded by the word cadet, and who it is you are looking for. Do you understand?"

If he was trying to intimidate us it was working. He had our attention.

As Kevin got up, Mr. Fletcher nodded in his direction and adjusted his glasses.

Kevin turned his head, and we locked eyes. His face scrunched up in confusion. I smiled and turned to give Mr. Fletcher my full attention. No way was I going to piss this guy off.

Throughout the next hour, our instructor lightened up a bit. He did not smile, but he gained our respect rather quickly. We were in school to learn to be future police officers. We needed to have thick skins. He discussed crime scene investigations, and explained that by the end of the semester we would be investigating a crime scene. I smiled because this was exactly what I wanted to do.

Once class was over, I made my way down the hall. Kevin had already taken off and was no longer in my view. I rounded the corner, and there he stood, black backpack thrown over his shoulder, his brown hair cut shorter than I'd ever seen it, but he still looked good. Was there anything he could do that would not make him look ... like him?

He wrapped his arms around me. "I can't believe you're here."

"Are you happy to see me, Finney?"

He laughed at me addressing him by his last name. He covered his face with his hands and shook his head.

"I don't think I made a very good impression on my first day." He shook his head as if shaking away the past hour. "I can't believe you're here, and you didn't call me to let me know. After all that time I spent trying to convince you to go to school with me and here you are."

"I decided kind of last minute."

"What made you decide to enroll?" His smile was now cocky. "Something I said?"

"Social work doesn't have an indoor firing range."

His smile dropped, his face now blank. "You make a good point. Well, I'm glad you're here, Jones. What class do you have next?"

Hearing him call me Jones was weird. "Gym."

"Me, too. It isn't just any gym class, you know. It's for law enforcement professionals."

"Rent-a-cops?" I said, with a laugh.

"Funny. You know you're making fun of yourself, right?"

I shook my head, but he was right. The rest of the college laughed at our polo shirts and uniforms. First year law enforcement students wore the polos and second years wore actual uniforms that looked identical to police uniforms. We were cops in training, but the community viewed us more like wanna-be cops. We needed to have thick skin, so I was not too worried about it.

The gym was on the opposite side of the college.

Kevin adjusted the shoulder strap on his backpack as we walked. "It's been a very long time. What's new?"

"I know, we sort of lost touch, didn't we? What happened to you last summer?"

"I did summer school so I could get ahead on my generals. I also worked security full-time. Trying to get some experience."

"That's great," I said, with little enthusiasm. He could have called or texted or sent a damn email. He was hiding something. "It's not just about not coming out to the lake. You stopped calling and texting. It's like you cut me out of your life."

"The phone works both ways, Lyndsey, you know. I can't believe you didn't tell me you were going to school to be a cop. You knew I'd be here." He opened the gym door and then turned to let me go in first. "Even if you found out last minute, you should have told me. It hurts."

A bunch of cadets were already in the gym, but they were all chatting in circles, not paying any attention to Kevin and me.

"Kevin, your dad died, and you didn't even call me. I had to hear it from my brother who was also pissed since we both missed his funeral."

His face turned stone cold. "I'm sorry."

He walked away. All I got was an apology? No reason at all? I deserved some kind of explanation.

His body language changed at the mention of his father.

He walked away and joined a large group of cadets chatting in a circle in the gym, and started talking to them, his back to me. I stood there all by myself until the teacher joined us and listed school expectations and rules. Kevin did not look at me the rest of class.

Luckily, this gym teacher was a lot less intimidating and admitted right away he was not a police officer, just a gym teacher that taught physical education to law enforcement students.

We partnered up for stretching. I ended up with a guy with horrible body odor. I mean horrible. I tried to breathe through my mouth as I pushed on his back to help him stretch, as instructed. He did not seem very excited to have me as a partner either.

This gym class had only one other female ,and she partnered up with Kevin right away.

She batted her eyelashes and fell all over Kevin throughout the hour. They walked ahead of me after class, as we all made our way back to the law enforcement department.

A familiar voice echoed down the hallway. Not until she was in Kevin's arms did I recognize her. Tracey? She was wearing a polo shirt. My heart fell. This was going to be a long two years.

She kissed Kevin on the lips and then our eyes met.

"Laura, right?" she said.

"Actually, it's Jones," I said.

"Oh, right." She rolled her eyes. "Did you follow Kevin to law enforcement school? That's so cute. Isn't that cute, honey?"

She tilted her head, and gave me a sympathetic look.

Kevin stepped in between us. "She didn't follow me. She's a better shot than anyone I know, and her dad is a cop. It's in her blood." He looked back at me and winked.

"I ... have to go." I walked past them and up the stairs.

He was confusing me with his mood swings. One minute he was mad and ignoring me, the next minute he was standing up for me and winking? Who was he? Did I know him at all?

One spot was open on the couch, next to a handsome guy who looked way too much like Zac Efron. Intimidating yet intriguing. I sat down next to him. "Is it okay if I sit here?"

"Be my guest."

"Great," I said, putting my bag down in front of me. "I'm Lyndsey Jones."

He nodded. "Zachary Johnson."

"No way."

He shot me a confused expression. "What?"

My face grew hot, and at that moment Kevin happened to be coming up the stairs. I looked back at Zachary as if I hadn't seen him. "It's just that you look an awful lot like Zac Efron. Has anyone ever told you that? And, well your name is Zachary. It just caught me off guard, that's all."

He grinned. "Actually, I have heard that. Although if I were him, I wouldn't be here. He's famous and too good for this modern life."

"True."

Kevin sat down on a chair off to my right, where he could see me perfectly. Our eyes connected, and he turned away. Was he jealous?

"Are you from the area?"

"No, the Cities. My wife and I moved here because I wanted to go to the best law enforcement school in the state, and she got a teaching job. We've lived here like a month now. You?"

He was married. This was probably for the best. I did not have to worry about him hitting on me or thinking I had a crush on him. Perfect. My heart was currently on strike anyway.

"That's great. I'm from Side Lake, lived here my whole life. You have Minnesota Statutes at eleven with Mr. Hanson?"

Zachary nodded. "Sure do. I'm just glad it's not with Mr. Fletcher. He's a bit intimidating."

"Right. Do you know Mr. Hanson then?"

He shook his head. "No, but he's the director of the law enforcement program. Were you at the introductory meeting when he gave the big speech?"

"No, was it bad?"

"That's probably good that you weren't. His speech would put the fear of death in anyone, that's for sure. I think half the cadets dropped out after that speech. One of the guys there told me he's a great teacher and person, but he gives that speech to get rid of the students who aren't devoted to being a cop. No reason to waste their time, or his."

"Makes sense."

Kevin got up and walked over to us. His eyes met mine. "Do you have Minnesota Statutes now?"

I nodded.

"Walk with me?"

Was he asking or telling me? It had been over a year since I last saw him, and he did not even seem like the same person. Was he with Tracey? Did I care? Yes.

I said goodbye to my new, very hot, and married male friend. "Nice to meet you, Zachary. See you in class."

I walked beside Kevin. "Where's Tracey?"


"In the bathroom. She's a big girl. She'll find her way."

"I see. Are you guys dating now?"

He stopped and pulled on my arm. "We've been together a few months. Nothing serious. We worked together doing security and we got close. I'm sorry I didn't tell you."

"It's fine. I don't own you."

I sat down at the table in the back of the classroom, and he sat next to me. That would piss Tracey off. "Just add it to the long list of things you don't tell me. Funny how you always said you didn't like her that way, though."

Tracey rounded the corner and came into the room with her nostrils flaring the moment she saw Kevin next to me. She let out a loud exhale and sat down on the other side of Kevin.

"Really, Kevin? Really?" She crossed her arms and turned away from him.

He shrugged it off.

The teacher came in, introduced himself, and said, "The seats you're sitting in will be the seats you continue sitting in for the rest of the semester."

This just keeps getting better.

*Now*

Two weeks later, Kelly's kids were released to their mother for a trial home visit. This was a case I would be passing on to an ongoing child protection worker due to all the concerns, but after safety planning and case planning, Kelly kept trying. Her UA's continued to be clean.

"I can't thank you enough for all you have done for my daughter. She is whole new person now. You don't know how much this means to me and her children," Ida said to me with tears in her eyes after Kelly's third clean UA.

"Don't thank me, she put in all the hard work. I can only do so much. Her new social worker will be here to continue helping her because the hard work isn't over."

She hugged me and I didn't want to pull away. I knew it was not professional, but she was so happy. "She's lucky to have you," I said before my last visit with her. I would still be checking in now and then with the ongoing social worker, but this was hopefully the last time I would be seeing Ida. Hopefully, I would never come across another report for this family.

Kevin was still investigating the case and charges were pending, which could take months. Kelly's progress made me smile at the thought. She had a good chance of staying sober, and she was taking her treatment seriously. And although she used, she did have a boyfriend, after all, who planted drugs in her home. She was working with the police to help catch him. She had realized he was not a good person for what he did, and not someone who should be around her kids. Sober, she was a completely different person who loved her kids. It helped so much that Ida was her mother and wanted nothing more than to help her daughter remain sober.

I had two options. I could visit Molly with Tracey, who was the only social worker not on backup or on call in our office. Everyone else was either out in the field, meeting with their own clients, or on vacation. The other option was to ask Kevin to meet me there and that was only on the off chance he was working today.

Of course, I picked Kevin. I'd rather have an awkward conversation about staying friends after we accidentally found ourselves in bed together after years of sexual frustration, or I could listen to Tracey make up lies about her relationship with Kevin or laugh at me.

This time Kevin was waiting for me outside Molly's trailer.

He even opened my door for me.

He stared into my eyes, his expression wary. "Are you sure you're ready for this?"

"Yes," I said like a sixteen-year-old girl. After it came out, I wanted to take it back. I cleared my throat. "Sorry, but yes, I'm ready."

He led the way to the trailer, and I followed close behind. He knocked on the door and Molly answered without a low-ball glass in her hand this time.

"You're back. What did I do now?" She was all attitude, and I was not surprised. She was her normal rude self and not the scarier version. My body relaxed, but I was still on guard.

"If you really don't know, we have a problem," Kevin said, as he bared his teeth.

"Come on, I didn't mean to hit her. I missed," she said, then looked at me coyly.

He took a step closer to Molly, his teeth clenched. "You ran after her with a baseball bat."

"I can't help it. I was angry. She took my kids away." She looked at her fingernails when she spoke.

I nodded. "I understand how hard that must have been, but my job is to make sure the kids are safe. It's never an easy choice. I want to work with you and your family by helping to get you all back together."

"I don't really have a choice. Do I?"

Kevin raised his chin. "You always have a choice."

She crossed her eyes and glared at me.

I would not let her think I was intimidated. "How do you feel about the kids staying with their dad for a while? Until you can get healthy?"

"I'm healthy right now!"

"Right, and that's really great, but you need to continue working on yourself before you can take care of your kids."

"Why do you get to make all the choices for my life? I have a lot going on, and Johnny is helping me stay sober. He's going to be my sponsor."

Kevin scrunched his eyebrows, and I did my best to keep a straight face.

"Is Johnny sober?" Kevin said.

She laughed, a little too loud and put her hand on Kevin's chest. He glared at her until she removed her hand.

"Johnny is always sober. It's what I love and hate about him."

I hardly believed her, but I could not do anything. The

kids were with their father, and I'd be handing this case over to an ongoing child protection worker, as well. We only passed over one case out of every fifteen to ongoing, but this week I was two for two.

"You guys can sit. You don't have to keep standing there, staring at me. I'm not going to throw anything at you, geez." She crossed her arms like a child.

"I'm fine standing," I said, not yet comfortable enough to sit down. My stomach was in knots, the fear intense again, even with Kevin.

"Go ahead and drug test me," she said, taking a step closer to me.

I took a step back, seeing flashes of the baseball bat coming at me from that day. I blinked hard.

"You need to keep some distance between the two of you," Kevin said as if he could read my mind. "Just for safety reasons, after the whole incident."

"I apologized, come on. I don't deserve to be treated this way in my own home."

"Lady, you're lucky Lyndsey didn't press charges against you. You should be thanking her for coming here today. She knows you need help, and she's willing to work with you after you attacked her. Have a little respect."

He had his thumbs underneath his vest when he spoke. He was angry and doing everything he could to keep his cool. Even sober, Molly was not getting it. She was nothing like us, and I needed to remember that. She was unpredictable.

*Then*

When the instructors were not in the room, Tracey had Kevin in a lip lock. No matter how many times she jumped on him and kissed him, the pain of watching them never got easier for me. I kept telling myself it would stop between them, but it never did.

Zachary quickly became my best friend. I told him about Kevin, and he listened to me complain about both Kevin and Tracey most days. He never gave me advice, he just listened, and that was exactly what I needed.

One Friday night, a bunch of us first years decided to get together for a party. Kevin volunteered his place. He gave us the address on Pill Hill, nicknamed because many of the Hibbing doctors lived in big houses on the hill. His place was probably even nicer than I expected. He likely inherited a ton of money after his father died and even though he deserved it, I was bitter. He was no longer my best friend. I debated even going to the party. Was it worth putting up with Tracey all night or watching them make out?

Zachary told me I was going whether I liked it or not. If

Zachary was going to be there, how could I not go? He could be my distraction.

Zachary picked me up at my house at his insistence, even though I lived twenty miles from town. We pulled up to the huge white house with a white picket fence and red shutters. The house was almost as beautiful as the Finney' cabin on the lake.

It did not take me long to get wasted. I was not driving so what did I care? This was the only way I could face the whole Tracey/Kevin situation. Just a little liquid courage.

A little over a year ago he assured me he had absolutely no attraction to Tracey. Did he think I was dumb? I saw it all along. He thought he was fooling me, but I saw right through it.

"You ready for this, Jones?"

I shot Zachary my best smile, smoothed out my pink blouse and ran my fingers through my hair. "As ready as I'll ever be, Johnson."

Before we had a chance to knock, Kevin opened the door. The minute he saw me he grinned, but then he saw Zachary, and the grin disappeared.

"Johnson," he said with a nod.

Zachary nodded back. "Nice place you have here."

Once inside, I gawked at the beauty of his house. The kitchen to our right had granite countertops and stainless-steel appliances. Tongue and groove floors covered the entryway, and the walls were all cedar and smelled amazing.

We took off our shoes, and followed Kevin into the living room where a few cadets were already gathered. I smirked when I saw the white carpets. How long before the carpets were ruined at a party? Then again, that's what maids were for, I guess. Must be nice to be that rich.

"What can I get you both to drink?"

"Vodka cranberry for me, please," I said with a smile.

"I'm driving, so I'll just have a pop," Zachary said.

"Sprite okay?" Kevin looked a bit relieved that Zachary was not drinking. He was very strict about drinking and driving, as expected.

After everyone arrived, Kevin made a speech about how if you drink, you stay. No exceptions. No one argued with him. The house had plenty of rooms.

Tracey was the last to show up with her dark winged eyeliner, short blonde hair, and tiny red dress that left little to the imagination.

The music was all nineties throwback, and I loved it. Shania Twain to Garth Brooks, Madonna, Destiny's Child, and Beastie Boys got me to my feet. Tracey was in charge of the music and although she was not my favorite person, I danced along with her choice of music.

About a dozen cadets showed up, three being women. The odds were in my favor that I would get hit on. Zachary and I danced, but he was a perfect gentleman, and I was grateful. He was married and that meant something to me. But by ten, I had no care left. I was hammered.

Once *Bring me to Life* came on, I decided I was a soloist. I sang it as loud as I could, and everyone surrounded me. I didn't have a care in the world. I drank to the point of no Kevin and Tracey, and it worked. I was down on the floor using my theater background to put on a show. Everyone clapped when I finished, but whether they were impressed or proud of me for putting myself out there, I neither knew nor cared.

I remember grabbing Kevin and pulling him onto the middle of his living room with me. Everyone was dancing, including Tracey. Zachary had distracted her. He was by far the hottest guy at the party, other than Kevin.

I was drunk enough not to see what Tracey was doing, but I no longer cared. Kevin and I were singing to each other and then a slow song came on and Gilley pulled me away from Kevin. Gilley was not bad looking, but he was a little too Robo Cop for me. His posture was perfect, his muscles big, and did he even have a neck? His body was stiff, and the guy kept stepping on my feet, so I put my feet on his and leaned in closer. I laid my head on his shoulder.

"I must tell you that solo you did earlier gave me goosebumps. Where did you learn to sing like that, Jones?"

I laughed, but I was a bit too dizzy to keep upright. I tried to focus on his face, but that last Jag bomb put me over the edge. My stomach was a little queasy. How long before I hit the porcelain throne?

"I did a little theater in high school, but you can't deny I was a hot mess out there." I was pretty sure my performance was an epic fail, and he was just trying to be nice or get lucky.

His hands slid to my lower back and that was when I felt hands peeling him off me.

"Come on, man," Gilley said.

I turned around to find Kevin standing there, shooting Gilley the most intimidating look I'd ever seen.

"Where's your girlfriend?" I said to Kevin. I laughed, nearly losing my balance. He put his arm around my waist and steadied me. Gilley walked away.

"Lyndsey, we need to get you to a bed. You're going to be sick tomorrow."

"It's Jones," I said laughing. Kevin was my best friend and now what was he even? "You know what Fin-ney," I said, emphasizing his last name.

He led me toward the back hallway. Was he even listening to me?

"Are you going to kiss me again? Your lips ... they are like so soft and dreamy. You know you were my first kiss?"

"I do."

"You were also my best friend until you ghosted me. But those lips—"

"Shush," he said and put his finger over my lips.

"No, you need to hear me out," I said, pointing in his face. "I'm in love with you, Kevin Finney, and you promised Tracey wasn't your—" I stopped as I felt the chunks rise in my throat.

He picked me up and leaned me over the bathtub.

I felt him behind me, holding my hair back as I vomited and vomited until there was nothing left inside my stomach.

I woke up on a couch somewhere in the basement, maybe? A warm body snuggled behind me.

Was I dressed? I pulled at my clothes, relieved they were still on. Who was behind me? I rolled off the couch and fell on the floor, hitting my head on the end table.

Kevin jumped up behind me. "Lyndsey, are you okay?"

I held my head as the pain spread all over. My stomach burned, and I was so dizzy.

"I think so."

He laughed as I looked him up and down to make sure he was fully clothed.

He pulled at his shirt. "What?"

"Nothing, I'm just glad we're both dressed. Why are we on this couch? Together?"

"I'm sorry. You had a bit too much to drink last night and I was worried about you. I wanted to make sure you were okay. I guess I fell asleep." He ran his fingers through his hair. He forgot I was his best friend for how long, and I knew his nervous ticks.

"Why are you so nervous then? Tracey going to find out you slept with me?"

The idea was funny until I saw her turning the corner and heading our way.

"There you are Kevvy. Why are you two down here? Did you sleep together?"

The high tone of her voice had me reaching for my ears. It hurt, it hurt. "Will someone please turn her off?"

She cocked her head and shook it at me. "Are you kidding me?"

Her hands were now on her hips.

Kevin threw his hands up in the air. "Nothing happened. She was sick and I was making sure she was okay, I promise."

She made an annoying pouty lip face at him. "What about me? I was sick, too. Why didn't you comfort me?"

Did she care or even realize she sounded like a five-year-old child having a tantrum in a toy store when she did not get what she wanted? This was who Kevin wanted to be with?

Her voice continued to rise, and I plugged my ears and snuck past them and upstairs to hopefully find Zachary. I wanted to go home, shower, and vomit in the comfort of my own home. Where the hell was he?

If the pain in my head would go away, I vowed never to drink again.

I gave up looking for Zachary and grabbed a banana off the counter. The sound of a grown man whining had me walking into the living room, and there on the floor was Zachary. He had a black eye and just one shoe on.

I ran over to help him up. "What happened?"

He held his hand over his eye. "I went looking for you last night and found you in the bathroom vomiting, with Finney holding back your hair. I decided I would lay down on the bed and sleep for a bit. Well, I guess Tracey thought I was Finney, and crawled in next to me and when I woke up and tried to climb over her to get off the bed, she grabbed her purse and hit me with it. She claims she thought I was a stranger. She's a bit crazy, if you ask me. Hot but definitely crazy.

"Did you put some ice on it?"

He hung his head. "No, Jones. This is as far as I got. She ran downstairs, and I just wanted to find you and go home. My wife is going to kill me. I don't know how I will explain this to her."

He would be in big trouble and right now I was in no shape to help him make up a better story, because every time I took a breath, I felt like I was going to be sick. I just wanted to go home.

Did Finney really take care of me and hold back my hair? How disgusting. Why would he do that? Monday would be rough during inspections at seven in the morning. Tracey would be giving me death glares. Like it or not, Kevin was her boyfriend now and no longer my best friend.

*Now*

Kelly passed her UA today and was clean, without a trace of meth in her system. Her supervised visits would start on Monday, and I was so happy for her. Ida was exhausted with the twins, but Mya was snuggled right up on Ida's lap when I showed up, reading a book. Ida was in her late 60s. Taking care of three kids under the age of seven was a tough job. But she loved them, and I was so glad she was not enabling her daughter like most cases I'd seen. So many times, the mother was the biggest problem.

At times the parents used drugs themselves, and that was how the drug chain started. Other times the parents would not believe their adult child could do any wrong. As parents, saying yes instead of no was easier, but Ida was not afraid to just say no. Her daughter was an adult, and she should know better. Ida loved her grandchildren, and she was fighting for Kelly by holding her accountable. With her support, Kelly had a good chance at getting better. She was motivated and it was easy to see the drugs impeded her parenting. She wanted to be a good mother. I had a feeling she would be successful.

Helping Kelly in a small way felt so good. Days like this I

loved my job. Although my conversation with Tracey in the back of my mind kept me from staying happy.

What were the odds I'd end up working with her? She was just pure evil.

"I think you need to let someone else be her social worker. I don't trust her," Kevin said, as he opened my car door for me.

"I can handle myself," I said, getting in.

The serious look on his face softened as he shut the door and leaned into my window.

"I know you can, I'm just looking out for you, okay?"

I chose not to respond as I backed out of the driveway and made my way to work.

"Why do you do this to yourself? We all know you're talented and smart and obviously very stubborn and fearless, but I think he's right."

I gasped at Maddy's remark. She was always supportive of my decisions and took my side. "You're taking his side? Seriously?"

Maddy put her water bottle in front of her face to block my direct view of her face. "I'm sorry, but you don't want me to lie, do you?"

I turned my head away, staring off at the lake. "Please be on my side right now. I need you to support me on this."

I heard her chair move as she got up and gently placed her hand on my shoulder. She had a way of calming me.

"After Ariel ... left this world ..." She cleared her throat Ariel's name made my arms break out in goosebumps. I still hurt thinking about her not running into my kitchen, and yelling out for her Auntie Lyndsey.

"I came to the realization that there are some fears we must confront head on and others we need to be smart enough to back away from," Maddy said. "I almost lost the love of my life due to my fears and anger. At the same time, I met a friend that I will never forget. Without Tim, I never would have found my way back to Brad."

"I know, and I'm so glad you let yourself be with the love of your life. But this is different."

She grabbed my arm. "Lyndsey, you're pushing Kevin away when all he's doing is reaching out to you. He wants to help you. He's not trying to be a jerk, and he doesn't think you can't handle being their social worker. He sees you've confronted your fears by going back to that house."

"I know, but—"

"That's the house you were assaulted at. I can't imagine how hard that must have been, but you also need to be smart about it. Know when to walk away. What that family needs is to start over with a new social worker."

It all clicked. I needed to make peace and walk away. She was right, I was not being vulnerable or weak. Both Molly and I needed a fresh start, and I had to say goodbye and move on, so she could do the same.

I hugged Maddy. Her shoulders stiffened and then she relaxed into my embrace, and held me tight.

"What was that for?"

I smiled. "Being honest enough to tell me the truth. You're right. I'll let my client know she needs a fresh start, and me going back there is only reminding her of who she was when she's trying to get better."

"Tomorrow is Friday and Brad, and I are having a barbecue. Please come over."

I never missed a barbecue at their house, unless I had to work late. "What are you up to? Why are you acting all weird?"

. . .

Maddy chewed on her lip as she looked at me. "If I tell you, you can't be mad at me, okay?"

"Maddy?"

"Fine. Brad invited Kevin over."

I let out a groan.

"I'm sorry. I just thought that maybe ... I thought the two of you need another shot. You are so cute together and obviously you're both still in love." After a moment of silence, she said, "Look me in the eye and tell me you don't still have feelings for him."

I couldn't and she knew it. She knew me better than anyone.

"You'll come?"


I stopped at Molly's house on my way home only to find a county car in her driveway. Tracey was just stepping into the car when I pulled up.

"What are you doing here?"

She was so sneaky. She had a reason, and it was not out of the goodness of her heart.

"Didn't Kate tell you? You're no longer the social worker for the Eiler kids."

"What are you talking about?" I had not told anyone I was giving up my client for her own best interest. I planned on telling Kate after I spoke with Molly.

"She didn't think you could handle it. She knew I wouldn't try to instigate anything, like you. Molly likes me. I've never had an issue. I guess Kate knows I'm better at calming people down."

I let out a laugh and then regretted it. I did not want to play down to her level. Ultimately, she was right. This was the reason I was here today. I faced my fears and went back to the home I was scared of, but I was ready to move on.

"Kate won't be happy when I tell her you came alone today. Maybe you'll finally get what you deserve. I don't think you're cut out to be a social worker."

I wanted to bite my lip, but instead I said, "At least I've never been fired from a job."

Okay, low blow. I was not proud of it, but a verbal slap was better than punching her.

"Hey, Lyndsey."

She got out of her car and put her hands on the roof with a grin. "I may have been fired but that was the same job they hired me over you."

"And then you were fired rather quickly for pepper spraying another officer. Isn't that right?"

"She was hitting on Kevin. She deserved it."

"You are crazy. You know that?"

"Bite me."

Another proud moment, as I flicked her off, got into my car, and drove away.

I wanted nothing more than to head to bed when I got home. I was exhausted, and forgot all about the barbecue until Maddy texted me to see when I was coming over. Lying that I was held up at work would not work because they were just a couple doors down and could pretty much look off their back porch to see my car in my driveway.

I touched up my makeup, slipped on my knitted teal sundress with the sixties flowers on the front, and walked over to my brother's house. Brad was there to greet me at the door and kissed my cheek.

"I was starting to think you weren't coming over. Come on in. We're out on the deck. Dinner is on the table."

I handed him a bottle of wine, and followed him onto the deck. Arms wrapped around me before I knew who I was hugging. Once she pulled away, I could not believe it was Mrs. Finney. I did not get a chance to talk to her at the wedding.

"How are you, Mrs. Finney? You look amazing," I said.

She grabbed onto my hand like she did not want to let go.

"I'm finally retired, and hoping to spend more time out at the lake after I sell the house in Rochester. We will be neighbors again. You sure look beautiful, Lyndsey."

"Take a seat," Maddy said. She set the salad on the table next to the food and sat down.

"You look so grown up and absolutely stunning," Mrs. Finney said. She turned around to look at Kevin, who was pushing in her chair. "Doesn't she look beautiful, Kevin?"

His eyes met mine and I felt my face heat up.

"The most beautiful woman in the world."

His words were a bit awkward. I held my breath until Maddy finally spoke. "I'm so excited you're moving back to the lake, Mrs. Finney. It hasn't been the same without you. Let Brad know and he can help put your dock in."

"Kevin could use the help. You know Troy, he isn't around much. That job he has keeps him traveling all over."

I took a sip of wine. "How is Troy liking married life? I can't believe he and Victoria ended up together. That's so great. It's obvious they're in love with each other."

"This is delicious," Mrs. Finney said after taking a bite of grilled lemon chicken. "She's perfect for him. They travel around together. She's a traveling blogger."

"They really are quite the couple, aren't they?" Maddie said. "Good for him."

Mrs. Finney looked right at me as she spoke. "I must admit, I'm a bit nervous now with Vincent gone and I'm retiring. You will come and visit, won't you, Lyndsey?"

"Of course," I said.

The rest of the dinner, she talked about her retirement and her plans to garden and kayak.

As we finished up and I put my dishes away, Kevin's mother followed me into the kitchen. She took my hand. "I see the way you and Kevin look at each other. Your mother and I always thought the two of you would get married. Don't let him get away, okay? You're meant to be. I think sometimes he worries about settling down because of how unhappy his father and I were." Her eyes filled with tears. "Lyndsey, please don't let him give up on love. You have always been the one. If the two of you would only see what the rest of us see."

"Oh, Kevin and I aren't—"

She put her finger to my lips. "Just think about it my dear, okay? That's all I ask." With that, she kissed my forehead like my own mother would, and she walked out the door.

I turned around. Kevin was staring at me. Had he heard the whole thing?

"The kayaks are out. Want to take them out?"

"Yes."

We walked to his parents' cabin and down to the lake.

"I wish I came out here more. The dock should be in by now."

"Me, too. I miss having you all next door."

The kayaks were turned over in the grass, and Kevin made no attempt to move toward them. He turned to me. "My mom is right, you know."

I looked down and let my hair hang in my face.

He lightly brushed my hair back and tucked it behind my ear, and lifted my chin with his hand.

"She is right about how beautiful you are, and she is right about us. Why haven't we ended up together yet?"

His eyes were gentle and sincere. How I missed this side of him. Like when we were teenagers.

"I don't know," I said, offering up a gentle smile.

"We were so close and then we just fell apart."

"Seems to be the story of our lives. Maybe it just wasn't meant to be."

We stared at each other for what seemed like forever.

"Or maybe it was."

He kissed me. His lips felt like silk on mine. My whole body felt warm, and our hands explored as the kiss went on and on. My heart felt so free, and the troubles in my mind vanished. Just Kevin and me. Here. Together again.

When our kiss broke apart, the anxious feelings returned. "I don't think this is a good idea."

"Give us a chance," he said.

I leaned in and kissed him again. This time my lips took the lead and pressed firmly into his. He let out a surprised moan, as if he wasn't expecting it. He kissed me back like I'd never been kissed before.

Our kiss took us down to the sand. It did not end until we were out of breath and had to come up for air.

We were sheltered from prying eyes thanks to the thick trees. No boats were on the lake to distract us.

Kevin ran his finger down my face. "I've missed you so much. Making love to you never felt like a mistake to me. It all felt so right."

Our lovemaking was far from a mistake, but I was afraid to admit it. Something was bound to happen to break us apart again.

*Then*

I stood in line with my hands at my sides, shoulders back, and my knees bent just enough to prevent them from locking, and me fainting in front of everyone.

The class commander took two steps, then stopped in front of the cadet a couple down from me, and stared him up and down. The assistant class commander followed him with a clipboard, marking the number of gigs each person received.

I could see him in my peripheral vision as he inspected Kevin, standing right next to me. Thirty seconds passed, and not one word. Then he moved on to me. If Kevin got a gig for his uniform, the class commander whispered it so low, I could not hear it over my heart beating heavily in my chest.

He took two steps, and pivoted in front of me. He was a good six inches taller than me, but I felt his hot breath on my face. His eyes scanned my head and then my shoulders. Left, right, down, left, right.

"You have a piece of hair on your left shoulder. Gig."

The assistant class commander scribbled something into his notebook.

He slowly moved his eyes over my shirt and stopped after what felt like twenty minutes.

"Your belt isn't aligned, gig."

I did not move an inch.

"Your pants are wrinkly, and your boots need to be shined more. Two more gigs."

He moved on and a loud noise almost had me looking, but I could not move. Not until everyone was inspected. We needed to remain perfectly still. I felt my body swaying. Out of the corner of my eye, I saw a person collapsed, and heard a bang! I now understood why we received a speech about not locking our knees during inspection. They did not want us to pass out.

Zachary and I headed to Grandma's in the Park, a restaurant down the road, after inspections. We had two hours to kill before class started, and I was in desperate need of a cup of coffee with a lot of sugar.

Zachary pulled his chair out and threw himself on it. "I got two gigs."

I shook my head. "I got four." I opened the menu. "What exactly are these gigs and how do we find out what we need to do?"

"You have to work them off. It's fifteen minutes a gig. Cleaning up garbage, or whatever is community service and approved by the class officers or teachers. You'll fill out a sheet with what you did to work them off and then you hand it in. You've got until inspections next week to do them."

"Or?"

"I don't really think anyone has tested out the or. You just do it."

The waitress brought us waters and took our orders. I ordered a coffee and hash browns.

"How do you know all this?"

He ran his fingers over the glass. "I ask the second years a lot of questions."

Kevin's head peeked into the restaurant. We locked eyes, and he headed right at us with a happy smile on his face. He pulled the chair out and looked at me. "Is someone sitting here?"

I shook my head.

I glanced at the entrance to see if Tracey was coming in behind him. I did not feel like dealing with her today.

Zachary also glanced to the doorway and then back at Kevin. "Where's Tracey?"

"It's just me." He looked a little distracted, not making any eye contact when he talked about her. Was there trouble in paradise? I could only hope.

Zachary took a sip of his coffee. "How did your first inspection go? How many gigs did you get?"

"None. How about you guys?"

"More than you," I said, shaking my head. "How did you not get any gigs? I double checked everything before inspection. I even had Zachary double check to make sure I looked perfect. Who knew our belts had to align perfectly with our zipper?"

He smiled, making my cheeks heat up. That smile got me every time. I couldn't have feelings for him. My feelings were just old habits. He was with Tracey now. Whatever friendship we had was hanging onto its last strings. Tracey did not want him to have anything to do with me, and he was not fighting her too hard.

"You'll get it," he said, after winking at me. "It just takes practice."

"How do you know all this?"

He shrugged his shoulders.

After I said it, I knew exactly how he knew. He researched

and figured it all out. He was always overly prepared. He probably should have been a doctor.

"Did you guys see Gilley pass out? Man, I can't believe he locked his knees," Zachary said. He shook his head and leaned back in his chair.

Kevin gasped. "That was Gilley? Is he okay? Sounded like his head bounced right off the floor."

"I saw him after, and he looked fine," I said. "I saw someone fall, but I didn't know it was him."

Zachary grabbed his phone and looked at it. He frowned. "Guys, I have to go," he said getting up. "Can someone pay for my food? Jasmine has a flat tire, and she's stranded on the highway. She has no idea how to change a tire."

Kevin stood up with him. "You want me to come with you?"

"No, sit down and enjoy my breakfast. We both don't need to be late for class and doing pushups. You know how Mr. Fletcher gets if we're late."

He looked right at Kevin and Kevin sat back down. "You're right. He'd kill me if I was late for a second time."

"We'll let him know what's going on," I said.

"Thanks."

He was out the door, and I was left with Kevin and awkward silence. He finally said, "Who is Jasmine?"

"His wife."

"Oh. I thought you two were kind of ..."

"No. He's just a friend. It's not like I have any other friends I can hang out with."

I felt a little bad as his face fell. "Yeah, I haven't exactly been myself lately. I'm sorry."

"I can't believe you and Tracey. I thought you said she wasn't your type."

He ran his fingers through his perfect hair that popped into place from all the gel.

"Yeah, about that."

"It's fine," I said as the waitress placed a plate in front of both of us.

"Bacon and eggs, perfect," Kevin said, picking up a fork.

The waitress came at the perfect moment to end our conversation.

"You need anything else?"

Kevin and I shook our heads.

"Okay, enjoy."

After she left, he locked eyes with mine. "Listen, Tracey is just a filler. After my dad died and my brother went to college, my mom fell apart. Tracey was there for me."

Nothing he said could have hurt me more. I wanted to be there for him, and how dare he use her? He really was nowhere near the same person he was a year and a half ago.

"Kevin, I couldn't be there for you because you never told me."

"I know. I thought everyone in Side Lake knew."

"You thought wrong. No one knew. Not even my parents."

He put his hands on the table and stared at them. "You know what my father was like. We didn't get along. I didn't know what to do when he died. I thought everything would be better when he wasn't around anymore. I didn't realize how much it would hurt."

I knew him well enough to know he was not lying. "I just wish you would have told me."

He nodded. "I wanted to. I didn't know what to say."

I put my hand on his hand. "I'm here for you. Just don't shut me out again, okay?"

His eyes teared up. "I can't believe how understanding you are being. The more time that went by, the worse I felt about not calling you. I'm sorry."

"Are you in love with her?" The words slipped out of my

mouth before I had a chance to think about what I was saying. But I could not take back my words.

He took a deep breath, unable to meet my gaze. "I don't know. I just don't know."

I shook my head.

"All I know is that my life is no longer the same without you in it. Please forgive me. Let me make it up to you."

"Okay."

"Can we start over?"

"How far back do you want to go, Kev?" My words came out so much ruder than I expected.

"I'm coming out to the lake today. Let me make a picnic lunch and we'll go kayaking. Maybe even have a bonfire like the old days?"

"And how will Tracey feel about that?"

He clenched his jaw. "She doesn't own me, Lyndsey."

"You could have fooled me."

He grabbed my knee, and I let out a loud squeal. "Kevin! What the hell."

He laughed. "I see you're still ticklish. I like to think I can still make you laugh."

His icebreaker changed our whole breakfast. We laughed and told each other about the past year. We missed so much of each other's lives, and it hurt.

"What do you think about the law enforcement program so far?"

I shrugged. "It's not so bad. I'm a little nervous about the red man suits. I have a feeling I'm going to get the crap beat out of me."

"I'll be by your side. Let's make sure to take defensive tactics together next year, okay?"

"Promise you will help me?"

"You got this. You just need to start believing in yourself."

. . .

181

We walked across the street and back to school. As soon as we made our way into the commons, Tracey came running at Kevin.

"Where have you been, Kev? I've been trying to call you, but you weren't answering."

She scowled at me when Kevin's head was turned.

"Just having breakfast, Tracey. Let it go."

She flipped her hair back and put it in a high bun.

I hated that he was with her. How could I make this friendship work if I had to deal with her jealousy every time I was with him? What did she even have to be jealous about? She was gorgeous and rich, and well, I was just me.

After class I made my way out to my car.

"Lyndsey, wait."

Tracey ran toward me.

I wanted to shut my door in her face, but she'd probably run after my car until I stopped. She was so used to getting what she wanted.

"I want to say that I'm sorry we got off on the wrong foot."

My eyebrow rose. I expected her to say many things, but never that.

"Okay?"

She grinned at me with a big, perfect toothy smile.

"It sounds like you and Kevin are friends again, and I can't change that."

Here we go.

"So, I want to you to know I can play this game, too. If you make one move on my man, I'll make your life a living hell."

I stood there staring at her. This was the real Tracey, but she still caught me off-guard with her threat.

"Got it?"

I laughed and laughed.

A look of absolute disgust crossed her face.

"Why are you laughing? I'm serious."

"We'll see," I said. Challenge accepted. We'll see who comes out the winner. She may be beautiful, but I was his best friend.

His text reached me when I was at home. *I can't make it for a picnic today. Raincheck?*

Tracey. Always Tracey.

*Now*

We agreed to take it slow. We would get to know each other again and not ruin what we had. We went on dates to Riverside and Bimbos restaurants. I took him out on my boat and we water skied. But I was waiting for it to fall apart. Good things did not happen to me.

He showed up at my house on the first week in August with a bouquet of daisies and lilies in his hand. He'd been working hard all day on cutting down the trees in between our houses. He had to work at six in the morning, so he was coming over for dinner before he headed to his actual house in town.

"They're beautiful," I said, as I took the flowers from him and put them in a vase on the table.

"I'm starting to see your cabin again when I look out of the window."

"It's a lot more work than I thought."

I took the burgers off the grill, and we sat out on the porch eating them while staring into the sunset.

"Move in with me."

His words came out of nowhere. Had I heard him right? "What?"

"Move in with me."

"In town?" He had to be kidding.

"Yes, in town."

"Kevin, it's too soon."

He sat up a little taller and moved closer.

"Lyndsey, we've known each other forever. Hell, I don't think I ever stopped being in love with you, even after all these years. It's not too soon. You're letting your fear talk."

I stood up, too nervous to sit anymore. "Kevin, if you knew me at all, you'd know I never want to leave the lake. I love it here. I have my own house. I'll never move into town."

He stood up, a concerned look crossing his face. He put his drink down on the table and placed his hand next to mine on the railing. "I thought you always wanted to move away."

I shook my head. "That was before I realized how much I love where I am. The lake, the people, the sunsets. Kevin, I'm happy here. You taught me that. You showed me many years ago that I was taking advantage of the nature that surrounded me. Of everything here."

"I did?" He was silent for a moment. "Okay then, I'll move out to the lake."

I turned around and grabbed our plates, anxious to get away.

He took them out of my hand and pulled me close. "What's wrong?"

"I'm not ready. I'm just not ready."

"But—"

"Listen, it's getting late. You have to work in the morning. Let's talk about it another day, okay?"

He kissed me on the cheek, and I walked inside. His phone rang before he made it to the door.

"Hello?" I heard him say, "Calm down, Tracey. Just calm down."

Silence.

"Did you call the police?"

I looked over the lake while he was on the phone. Tracey was calling him? I no longer felt bad about not wanting to live with him. He wasn't ready to move forward with me if he was still talking to Tracey. He'd never see she was a horrible person or how much she wanted to be with him again. I was battling her for him all over again. Nothing had changed.

"Okay. Call them. I'm on my way, okay? Don't cry."

He handed me his empty glass. "Listen, I have to go. Tracey had a break in, and she's really upset."

"But you aren't even on the clock," I said, in an angry voice I did not recognize. I did not believe a word she told him. She was lying and Kevin wanted to believe the best in her. Tracey would always come first.

"I know. I'm not going there as a police officer, but as a friend. She doesn't have anyone else."

I was being selfish, but I turned my back on him in a show that I was not happy.

"We'll talk more about this tomorrow, okay? I'm sorry but I have to go."

He tried to grab my hand, but I shook it off. "Goodbye," I said, and shut the door.

I watched him drive away through the curtains.

The tears ran down my face. If her house was actually broken into, and he was being the good guy by helping her, I would end up feeling like such a jerk. Why did I even care? Because Tracey was always the third person in my relationship with Kevin. She was around when we were teenagers and then again in college. She would never go away. How did I end up having to work with her and see her all the time? Even as an adult?

But jealousy was unlike me. I was scared because I was in love with him. Utterly and stupidly in love with him, and it scared me. What was I scared of? Maybe the wine was getting to me. I laid down on the couch and fell asleep. I would analyze my feelings tomorrow.

I called him around noon the next day, but he did not answer. I knew he was working so, I sent a text.

*ME: I'm so sorry about last night. Can I come over tonight after you're done with work so we can talk?*

*FINNEY: I'm getting done early. Come over around four instead. We need to talk.*

*ME: Sounds good.*

We need to talk? That sounded a little rude. But I had to stop reading too much into the text.

I showed up a little after four. His car was not in the driveway, but I knocked anyway.

To my surprise, the door opened, but Kevin was not standing at the open door. Tracey, in a towel with wet hair, smiled so wide it took my breath away.

"Hey, Lyndsey. What are you doing here?"

Had I ever seen Tracey that happy?

"I'm here to see Kevin, but I'm guessing he isn't here."

"Oh no, he's in the shower. When I heard the knocking, I

jumped out of the shower, but he's still in there. Do you want me to get him?"

I waved my hands. "No, no. I didn't realize."

She held her hand above the door and leaned on it.

"You didn't realize Kevin and I were back together? Well, it was inevitable we would end up together in the end. We agree our divorce was a mistake, and we can't live without each other. What can I say? I'm irresistible."

Breathe, Lyndsey, just breathe.

"You don't look so good, Lyndsey. You didn't really think Kevin liked you, did you? Aw, you're so cute, you know that? Yikes. Well, I'm getting a bit cold so I'm hopping back in the shower, Kevin's waiting. Toot-a-loo."

She shut the door, but I stood there, not moving an inch. My mouth was hanging open in shock. He asked me to move in with him yesterday. What the hell just happened?

I got into my car and drove down the street, then pulled over to cry. I tried calling Maddy, but she did not answer, so I sent her a text and then I called Kat. When life got hard, we still knew we could count on each other, no matter how many miles we were apart.

Kevin tried calling me multiple times until I finally turned off my phone. I was not ready to talk to him yet. He and Tracey could live happily ever after, for all I cared. The thought of having to see Tracey at work tomorrow was enough to make my blood boil.

Maddy showed up and gave me a big hug the next morning, which made my eyes water again. Just when I thought they were too dry to produce any more tears, they proved me wrong.

"Have you talked to him at all?"

I shook my head.

"Are you going to?"

"I'm not ready. I don't know how I can go to work tomorrow. I don't want to see Tracey ever again. She'll brag to her friends and rub it in my face. I don't think I can do it anymore."

"Lyndsey, you've been wanting to quit that job forever. You're always stressing about kids and worrying about something happening to them. I heard Mark and Amy are looking for someone to help clean cabins. Why don't you do that for a while and leave your job? It'll give you time to think about what you really want to do."

I shook my head. "I can't. I'm too worried about the children if I leave."

She rubbed my back with one hand. "That's the problem. You love too much. You're sensitive and empathetic, and that job is not for someone like you. It hurts you too much and gives you way too much anxiety. It's not for everyone, and I think you need to give yourself a break and let it go. Your job is replaceable, and I hate to say it but you are replaceable. You can't let it eat you up inside. It's just a job." Maddy hesitated. "And to be honest, I worry about you getting attacked again. You don't have any protection out there."

Everything she was saying was true. I did need to leave to save myself. I needed to trust that someone else could do my job and help the children on my caseload. This job was eating me up, and the stress was giving me headaches and stomach aches. I did not argue because I knew she was right. I took my job everywhere with me.

"You're right."

She blinked. "Did I hear you right?"

She never expected me to leave my job. I didn't either.

"I'll quit first thing in the morning. After everything that's happened, I'll ask that they don't make me wait a month."

"I think they owe you that," she said. "Why don't we put

in a movie and just chill? Not think about anything for the rest of the night.

"Only if we can watch *Bad Moms*."

"Deal."

# Now

I was home by noon, after quitting my job with full benefits and a great pension, but I had no regrets. I was choosing me. Mark hired me to clean cabin five, the creative cabin. Someone would be renting it until December, so he wanted me to clean it before the guy moved in.

I went straight to work at Pine Beach Resort, not wanting to think about anything except cleaning. Cleaning cleared my mind.

I'd been to Pine Beach many times. The resort was on the Sturgeon Lake chain, and right off McCarthy Beach Road. A small community of permanent campers lived there in campers from spring until fall. They swam, hung out at camp-fires by the beach, boated, and enjoyed everything else outdoors and lake related.

Amy, the owner of the Pine Beach resort, met me at her cabin and her teenage son, Dave, was out front planting lettuce in their garden.

"Lyndsey, how are you?" Amy wrapped me in a bear hug. "It's been too long."

Pine Beach was always so welcoming. People came from all over to stay in the beautiful cabins. Mark and Amy took a lot of pride in their resort, and they put a lot of time, effort, and love into it.

"I'm doing good."

Amy fired up her golf cart, and I hopped in next to her. "Dave, make sure to water the plants when you're finished, okay?"

Dave was on his phone. He quickly tucked it into his pocket, not wanting his mother to see he had been on it.

"I just remodeled cabins five and six. I think you'll like the new look."

I followed her into cabin five. A big window covered most of the wall, with a perfect view of the lake and boats tied to the dock. The big table was made of cherry oak. The cabinets matched. Books lined a bookshelf. I went over to take a look at the wide variety of genres.

"I was told back in the day, before Mark and I owned the resort that Mary Higgins Clark used to stay here sometimes in the summer and write books. That's why we call it the creative cabin. We have a young man who will be here in about an hour. He's a writer or maybe he's an editor. Anyway, he's staying until December and plans on working while he's here."

I took in the whole place, the desk by the window with a full view of the water, which would be a perfect spot for any writer to get inspired. The shower was newly tiled with beautiful stones, big and small. The deck outside had chairs to relax and take in nature, and the view. The cabins even had a fire pit out by the water for campfires. An indoor fireplace was perfect for the deer hunters and snowmobilers that came to stay. The resort had the most relaxing atmosphere for both the winter and summer months, and just the atmosphere I wanted to spend my days working in.

Was this man coming alone? If he was coming to write, he was probably coming alone.

Amy set a laundry basket on the floor next to the table. "Here's everything you need to clean. The sheets have already been washed, you just need to scrub the toilets and shower, dust, and clean the kitchen sink. Let me know if you have any questions."

"Thank you so much, Amy. I really appreciate it."

She smiled. "Are you kidding? We're family. The Side Lake family. We watch over each other, and I could honestly use the extra hands. We're booked solid through the holidays."

I turned up my music, and danced my way through the cabin cleaning until everything sparkled. I turned around to finish putting away my cleaning supplies. Ethan was standing there, looking at me. I jumped. We both laughed and I turned down the music.

"Sorry about that. You must be the writer or editor?"

"What?" He looked frightened by my words.

"Amy said a man was staying here who would be writing while he stayed in this cabin. She was excited since it's the creative cabin. I never expected it to be you. I knew you lived in New York, but you're a writer there?"

He laughed. "I do a little freelance writing. I guess I have so many good memories of this place as a child. I figured why not write from here? I don't need to be in New York to do my job. I miss it here."

"I get it. I left my job for a while myself. The stress was getting to me, and who doesn't like cleaning?"

"You are crazy. I don't like to clean, and I don't understand how it can give you joy."

"It's actually quite relaxing." I turned to leave, feeling more relaxed than I had in a long time.

"Lyndsey, wait," he said, coming toward me. "The next

JENNIFER WALTERS

time you talk to Kat, could you let her know I moved back? I would like to see her sometime."

"I will, but I can't promise it will help. She refuses to come back here."

He turned away. "I understand, but I had to try."

"I wouldn't stop trying if I were you."

## Then

Tracey won.

Kevin became a bit distant, and the school year flew by.

On a Monday morning, the teachers announced they would be picking the class officers. If interested, we needed to apply and write down which position we wanted. No one was really talking about it. Who was applying was kept hush hush.

I sat down on the couch to fill out my application, when Tracey and Kevin walked in.

"I bet she's filling out the application for class officer. As if she'd get it," Tracey said to Kevin, but loud enough for me to hear, as she strutted past me into the teacher's office. Her nose was so high in the air I wanted to ask her if she had a nosebleed. Instead, I bit my tongue.

Tracey had volunteered to help set up for the second-year crime scene processing classes, and to help set up targets for the indoor shooting range. I was not sure how she got it, but I tried not to care. She had the teachers all convinced she was this amazing person.

Kevin sat down next to me, a little too close to me after Tracey's nasty comments. He did not even try to defend me.

I covered my application with my notebook.

"I'm applying too," he said.

"Oh, so now you're talking to me? Only when she's not around? Don't you think it's weird that she won't even let you say hello or look at me? Why would you let her control you like that?"

He put his head down. "I'm sorry."

He avoided fighting with Tracey, and this was easier. I had to find a way to let it go. Things had changed between us, and we would never get that back.

"I figured you would apply. It's what you've wanted since we were teenagers."

He looked down at his hands. "You're right. Do you remember the day we first met? It's a day that has been engraved in my mind. The way you looked so cute, with your nose in your book and your grumpy little face."

He tried to tap on my nose with his finger, but I swatted him away and tucked my chin against my chest.

"Stop."

He listened, then broke the silence. "What position are you applying for since you already know which one I am?"

"Community Service Officer, if you must know." I couldn't help but snap at him. He needed to stop letting Tracey control him.

"You'd be good at that. We could spend the whole summer working together. It would be fun."

Kevin and me working together every day throughout the summer? Driving to the Cities to bring our cop cars to other programs, cleaning the shop where we kept the law enforcement cars. I would be so angry if Tracey applied.

"Is Tracey applying?" I had to ask. If she got the position, I would no doubt turn down my position. I could never deal with her that directly all the time.

"No. I don't think so. I told her I needed to do this

without her. She has some influence with the teachers, but I don't care. We got into a big fight over it." He leaned in close to me and in a whisper said, "As soon as I secure my position as class commander, I'm breaking up with her. She won't leave me alone, follows me everywhere, and she's so bossy."

"You're just now realizing that?"

He laughed. "Listen, I'm having a few people over tonight. Why don't you bring Zachary? It won't be a big crazy party or anything. Just a get together with a few people from the program. Celebrate the last weekend before we're officially second year law enforcement students. What do you say?"

I had nothing better to do so why not. "Is Tracey going to be there?"

"I'd like to say no, but I'm sure she will be."

Say no. "Yes, we'll be there."

I should have learned my lesson the last time I got wasted at Kevin's house, but I didn't. This time Tracey would not leave Kevin's side, and I slam down drink after drink. We had a great time dancing and playing quarters, which I was no good at.

And then I woke up wearing only my bra and underwear, with no memory of how I ended up in bed with Zachary. I looked under the sheets, and confirmed he was also only in his underwear.

"Shit! Zachary wake up!"

I had to shake him until he finally opened his eyes.

"Jones?" He yawned, scratched his head, and then I saw the oh crap look as he jolted up in the bed with wide eyes. "Did we? Please tell me we didn't ..."

I jumped out of bed, searching for my shirt and pants. "I don't know. Why don't I remember anything?"

I was off balance, and caught myself on the wall after

almost tripping over my own feet. I was never drinking ever again.

"My wife is going to kill me!"

"Calm down, I don't think we slept together. We couldn't have. No." The truth was, I had absolutely no recollection, so I was not really sure of anything.

"No. No. No. I'd never cheat on my wife," he said.

He was fully dressed now with tears in his eyes.

"I don't think we did. I really don't. Do you remember anything?"

He pinched the bridge of his nose. "I had one drink, one. My wife will never forgive me. It's impossible I would get that drunk from one drink."

"Don't tell her. You don't even know we had sex. There's no reason to upset her if we didn't do the deed."

I was right and he knew it. Whatever happened we would never know.

"You're right. I feel awful."

He put on his socks and typed something into his phone. It immediately started ringing.

"It's my wife."

"Breathe, Zachary. Nothing happened. You said you had one drink, right? Someone put something in your drink."

He put on a smile and answered it. "Hey, honey. I just woke up and I'm on my—"

He went silent and stood there, not moving an inch. He turned his head in my direction and put a finger to his lips to quiet me. "Hang on, I'll put you on speaker. You said I sent you a picture?"

I stared at his phone with him. We both stopped breathing.

"Are you there, Zachary? How dare you? It's over."

"No, no. That wasn't me, please, honey. Let me explain. Nothing happened."

"Get your shit out of my house, and you can find your own place."

He did not argue and how could he? We kept staring at the photo of the two of us in our underwear on the bed with my hand in his underwear.

"How could you have taken this picture?" I said. "It's not possible. We were both passed out, clearly. You sure you only had one drink?"

"Yes, I'm positive. I need to go," he said in a panic.

"We were set up, Zachary. Your wife will believe you, I know she will."

He did not answer me, and I did not try to stop him. He was gone.

I had no ride home.

"Rough night?' Tracey asked, coming from behind me. She had a huge smirk on her face as she raised an eyebrow at me. It was her. Of course, it was her. How could Tracey would do something so evil without a bit of remorse?

"It was you," I said, pointing in her face.

She brushed my hand away. "I don't know what you're talking about."

Oh, she knew.

"Who else did you send that picture to?"

"No one, yet."

I walked out the door and called my mother for a ride. This was war.


On Monday, Kevin was in the commons, studying on the couch all by himself.

"Kevin, can I talk to you?"

He looked up at me and when he saw my expression, he closed his book.

"What's going on? Are you okay? Is it your mom? Your dad?"

I shook my head and put my thumb in my mouth, chewing on my nail.

"You know the night of your party? Well, I woke up in bed with Zachary."

He turned away. "Tracey told me, but I thought it wasn't true. He's married, Lyndsey. Married! I can't believe you would do that. You were both that drunk?"

His words struck me. "Kevin, come on. You know me better. Tracey's lying."

"Don't blame Tracey," he said with a glare. "You messed up big time. You better hope they aren't getting divorced."

"Seriously? Kevin, Tracey took a picture and sent it to Zachary's wife. She's out to get me."

"She wouldn't do that. She didn't do that. Don't blame Tracey for your actions." He stood up, his hands shaking.

"Kevin, please, you have to believe—"

"Jones, Finney, I'm glad you're both here. I need to talk to you," Mr. Hanson said.

He could not have come at a worse time.

I had no choice but to breathe and follow Kevin into Mr. Hanson's office.

"Sit down," he said, pointing at two chairs in front of his desk. He sat on the corner of his desk.

"You two are my top students, and I couldn't be prouder of your progress. You had the best interviews of all the cadets, and I want the both of you to represent the program as class commander and assistant class commander."

I should have been happy and proud, but instead I could not even think about his words. Everyone hated me and thought I slept with a married man. This was going to be a long year. I would have to hold my head high because I knew the truth, and Zachary knew the truth. Even his wife believed him after I showed up there and explained everything that happened. It took some convincing, but she trusted Zachary, and she knew deep down he would never do that. Not even drunk. I knew it, too.

"I was surprised to see that you applied for the assistant class commander position, Kevin. You seemed so sure about being the class commander in your interview. I respect that, and it's obvious the two of you planned this since Jones here applied for class commander."

Kevin and I exchanged confused glances.

"Congratulations, Jones. You are the first female class commander in ten years. What an accomplishment. You earned it." And then he shook my hand.

We walked out, and Kevin would not even look at me. By the time we got to class he said, "How could you?"

I had no answer. How could everything go so wrong so fast?


The year went by at a snail's pace. Kevin and I made it through the year with hardly a word said to each other, unless we had to speak for some reason. Our friendship was over, and he and Tracey seemed more in love than ever.

To say he hated me was an understatement. He'd get up and walk away when I was near. He stopped answering my calls and texts, and I learned to stay far away from him. We worked the summer together driving cars from colleges and helping with the summer skills program. He was cold and I ignored it the best I could, but my heart was broken.

After we graduated, I applied to the Chisholm Police Department. As luck would have it, I did not get the job. Tracey, however, did. Could my life get any worse?

Soon after, I decided my true calling was social work. I'd seen what Kevin had been through with his dad, and I wanted to help children like him. No matter how much he hated me, I never stopped loving him. I hoped one day he would see Tracey for who she truly was.

*Now*

I took the cleaning supplies back to Mark and Amy. Maddy was running down the path in my direction.

"Maddy?"

She was out of breath. "I've … been … looking …"

"Slow down, breathe."

She breathed deeply and took her time until she could speak without panting. "Kevin came over to the house looking for you."

"I don't care," I said and walked away.

"Lyndsey, you need to hear this. I promise you'll be glad you did."

I crossed my arms. "You know I'm done with him, right? I was hoping to never hear his or Tracey's names ever again. Please make this quick, you're ruining my meditative state."

"Kevin came over because you weren't answering his calls."

"Did you tell him he's a jerk, and he should go back to Tracey?"

"I did."

I was even more annoyed. Why had she come all the way here to tell me that? I did not want to hear about it anymore.

"And ..."

"And he said after Tracey's house was burglarized, she was devastated so he told her she could stay at his house a couple days until the windows were fixed and the locks were changed."

"Yeah, I figured that she was staying with him when I showed up at his house and found her in a towel. He was waiting for her in the shower!"

Maddy was still trying to catch her breath so she could explain something more. The wait was killing me.

Finally, I said, "Spit it out, Maddy!"

She held out a hand until she could finally speak. "Okay, that's the crazy part. Kevin cringed when I mentioned the whole shower incident. He swore up and down he never took a shower with her. He never texted you to come see him either. He was at work until six. He had left his personal phone at his house because he doesn't usually have it on him while he works. He didn't think anything of it at the time. I told him he needed to check his phone. Lyndsey, all his texts to you were deleted and your number was blocked."

"Blocked? Why did he block me?"

She groaned. "That's what I'm trying to tell you, he didn't. Tracey went to great lengths to split the two of you up. She was at his office that day you texted him, too, and he's pretty sure she's the one who wrote you back. Don't you see? He isn't with her, and he hasn't been since the divorce! He wants to be with you."

My heart was beating so hard in my chest. I would hunt her down and confront her. Enough was enough. I pulled my keys out of my pocket.

"Where are you going?"

"To Tracey's," I said, through clenched teeth and tunnel vision.

"What are you going to do?"

"Get to the bottom of this. I quit my job and she set me up. She's an adult and the games end now. Was Kevin going to her house when he left?"

"I don't know. He was pretty upset but got called out on the radio and had to go. He was a mess about the whole thing."

"I doubt he's innocent. He always believes her crap. She's like an annoying mosquito always buzzing around my head and bothering me, and I'm going to put an end to it."

"Lyndsey, be careful," she said, as she shut my car door. "Call me, okay?"


Her little red car was in the driveway when I pulled up. I rang the doorbell and the minute I saw that perfect smile, I wanted to swat it right off her face.

"Lyndsey, what a surprise."

"We need to talk," I said, in a voice that made her eyes bulge in fear.

"Sounds like a you problem," she said, turning away.

I stood in her front entry way. "Where's Kevin? You're dating now, aren't you?"

Her face turned red.

"Why are you blushing, Tracey? You think we're stupid and wouldn't figure out you were texting me and set this all up? That you blocked my number so Kevin and I couldn't talk to each other?"

She smirked. "It took you long enough."

"What's your problem with me?"

She pointed her finger at me. Her embarrassment now turned to anger in an instant.

"If not for you, Kevin would be with me. I always came second to you. I thought this time you would finally get the hint. I don't even know what he sees in you. I thought when I erased your community service officer application in college and changed it to class commander and when I changed his class commander application to assistant class commander, that would be enough, and it was for a while. I thought putting a pill in you and Zachary's drinks and putting you in Kevin's bed at that party in college would be enough to finally end this thing between the two of you, but still you somehow found each other. I thought when I applied for the Chisholm Police Department after we graduated and I told them you were a drunk so you wouldn't get the job, that would have been enough, but no."

"That was you? You really are crazy."

A shadow moved in the open window behind her. Kevin was overhearing everything she was saying.

"I'm not crazy. I'm a woman in love! Except you keep getting in the way, and I'm sick of it. Once I found out the two of you were at your house having sex on the beach, and getting way too cozy for my liking, I knew I had to do something about it. He was my husband, Lyndsey, mine. He chose me."

My eyes widened in horror. "Please tell me you didn't lie to Kevin about your house being burglarized so you could try to seduce him."

"It almost worked, too, but he'll never believe you, Lyndsey. All I have to do is turn on the tears, and he will believe me over you. He always has and always will."

"Not anymore."

"How could you lie about someone breaking into your house? You went to school to be a cop. What about honesty?"

"Honesty? You can't get ahead with honesty. You would have gotten the job and the guy, if I wasn't there to make sure that didn't happen. If I were honest, I would be like you. No thank you. You didn't get that job for a reason. I did. Can you imagine if you were a cop? You couldn't even cut it as a social worker."

"I was a great social worker and you've always been jealous. You know I would have made a better cop than you. That's why you had to lie to make sure I didn't get the job. You're the one who couldn't cut it as a cop."

"Technically, I got fired for standing up for myself. It was just a little pepper spray. They took everything so personally."

I rolled my eyes. "Sure. "

"It's true. I never should have been fired for that."

"If that's what you really think." What a laugh. She wasn't exactly the type of person I would want to come to my rescue.

"You are just jealous because Kevin married me and not you. You've always been jealous."

"He also divorced you. I'm guessing he already figured you out."

"He believes anything I say. If I wanted him back, I could get him back."

"I highly doubt it."

She crossed her arms. "I'm going to call him right now and tell him you broke into my house and threatened me. You will see who he believes." She took her phone out and started scrolling.

"Good luck with that."

As if on cue, two officers knocked on the door.

"That is probably him now," she said, flipping her hair behind her shoulders and adjusting her skirt before she opened up the door.

"Tracey Hogart, you are under arrest for falsely reporting a crime and insurance fraud. You have the right to remain silent."

The police officers cuffed her behind her back, but not with out a struggle.

"Get your hands off me. I did nothing wrong. I want a lawyer." She screamed out in frustration until she saw Kevin standing by the door shaking his head at her. "Kevin, help me, they're arresting me. I did nothing wrong. Stop them. Stop them, Kevin!" Her voice got louder when he showed no sign of trying to stop them.

"I think you've fooled me one too many times, Trace. We have video evidence from your neighbor's camera of you throwing a rock at your own window and breaking your own things," Kevin said.

"That's bullshit. I was nowhere near my house that night."

"Tracey, stop, I saw the tape and it was clearly you. Clear enough for a judge to sign a warrant."

"Oh, Kevin, you know I did it for us, right? I didn't want you to end up with her again. She's a horrible person," she said, tilting her head in my direction.

If she was going down, she was going to do everything she could to make sure he didn't end up with me. Classy. I was enjoying every minute of this.

Kevin scowled. "You need help, you know that? Guys, take her away."

She leaped at Kevin and a female officer pepper sprayed her. "Payback is a bitch," she whispered in Tracey's ear, loud enough for me to hear.

I pursed my lips and chuckled deep down. It was definitely the officer Tracey pepper sprayed. Funny how karma always tends to find us.

Tracey kicked and screamed but they led her away.

I locked up her house and walked out the door to find Kevin standing there.

"That officer finally gave Tracey her karma, huh? Did you hear what she whispered?"

He laughed into his hands and rubbed his eye. "Yeah, that would be Officer Kenzington."

"Oh, she told me about her. It's about time she got her payback."

"I owe you an apology."

"Can we not do this here, please?"

He smiled. "Meet you at your house? I have to make a statement and then I'll be there."

I nodded and made my way home. Was this the best or the worst day? Maybe both. Tracey finally came clean, and she would lose her job. A part of me felt bad for her, but the other social workers would be better people without her around to manipulate and destroy everything in her path.

The lake was beautiful this time of day, with the boat traffic building up the waves. I sat down at the end of my dock and dangled my feet in the water.

I heard his footsteps and my heart beat faster.

He sat down next to me. "She sure had me fooled," he said.

"I can't believe she has been fooling us all these years," I said.

His hair was blowing in the wind, his aviators pushed up on his head. He had to be the most handsome police officer I'd ever seen.

"We kept falling for it. You'd think our friendship was stronger than that," Kevin said.

I splashed my feet in the water. "I guess it wasn't. That or we never thought she was smart enough to pull off something like that."

He laughed. "I knew about the Chisholm Police Department but by the time I found out, she was already fired. The class commander position was news to me. I owe you an apology."

"It's not your fault. I told you I wasn't applying for it, and then I got it. I understand you must have been pretty mad.."

"But it wasn't true," he whispered, his words getting caught in the wind. "The worst was what she did with you and Zachary. Luckily his wife never found out or that would have been bad."

I gave him the side eye. "Are you kidding me? She slapped me when I tried telling her the truth after that night. Luckily, she finally believed me. Tracey sent her half naked pictures of me and him in bed together. It was bad."

"Wow, I had no idea. What a horrible woman. And I married her," he said with a laugh, shaking his head.

"But you were also smart enough to divorce her."

He put his arm around me, and we sat there together breathing in the fresh air and listening to the roar of boat engines and the waves coming in. The laughter of families having a good time tubing caught both of our attention as we watched them come in our direction. We waved at the boat when it came closer and they waved back, including the children on the tube.

"You're right, life on the lake is amazing. I don't think I'd ever want to live in town again either. It's just so beautiful out here in the middle of nature."

"Sounds exactly like a friend of mine that helped me fall in love with the lake when I was just a teenager," I said.

"Oh really? Sounds like a smart guy. Is he good looking?" He raised an eyebrow at me and smiled.

"He's alright. You hungry? I can make us a sandwich."

He jumped to his feet and held out his hand to help me up.

"I am feeling a bit hangry," he said.

"You haven't changed one bit." I put my hand in his

pocket to grab his wallet and phone, and then I pushed him into the water. A big splash of karma drenched my shirt.

We both laughed, and I took off toward shore before he could pull me in. Our phones would both be going into the water if he caught me. Something fell in the sand. I turned back to see what it was.

It was my phone. It started ringing.

"It's Kat," Kevin said as he answered my phone and put it on speaker phone.

"Give me my phone," I yelled playfully as I jogged toward him. I stopped to listen as he held it out of reach.

"Hi, Kat," he said turning his back to me so I was unable to grab my phone from him. "It's Kevin Finney here. Long time, no see."

She let out a loud sob, and his eyes widened in panic. "Kevin, I'm sorry but I need to talk to Lyndsey. Is she there?"

He held the phone out to me.

"I'm here, Kat, are you okay?"

The line went silent. I put it to my ear. "Kat, Kat," I said, no reply. I called her back as I walked toward my house, but the phone kept ringing behind me.

I looked to the side of the cabin, and there stood my best friend in the whole world. I thought I was hallucinating at first.

"Kat, you're here? What are you doing here? I thought you'd never come back. Are you okay?" I was in total shock. I thought she would never return. She wanted nothing to do with her mother, and never wanted to see her ever again. She made that very clear.

"I told you I'd come back over my mother's dead body and guess what?"

"Oh, Kat! I'm so sorry." She hated her mother, but I knew she did not want her to die.

She hugged me tight, and we cried together. As we separated, she looked over my shoulder at Kevin.

She wiped her eyes. "Here we are again. She's my best friend, Kevin. I thought I told you to back off years ago."

"It's great to see you again, too, Kat meow. If only Ethan was here."

Kat wiped her eyes and laughed. "I'm pretty sure he isn't living in Minnesota anymore. I don't think I would recognize him if I saw him."

"About that," I said.

# Acknowledgments

The Turtle Creek Series was created as my first series based out of the beautiful lake town of Side Lake. After writing Greenrock Road, I knew the lake was where my heart is. Not only is it beautiful, but the community is full of the kindest people. Thank you to the whole town of Side Lake for all your support. It is my favorite place to be, especially in the summer.

Deepest appreciation goes to my husband, Owen, who has not only supported me in my writing journey since day one, but read and reread every book I've written so far. Also to my daughter, Alexis, who reads every book out loud with me and helps me find the plot holes before I send it off to my editor. You both have no idea how much it means to me.

Thank you to my amazing editor, Shirley Frederick, who has been with me since book two. Without you, my book would not be what it is. Thank you.

Much thanks to my whole family and my friends for all your love and support. For going to book signings with me and supporting me as I continue living my dreams.

With special thanks to law enforcement and all the amazing social workers out there. Your job is not easy and what you do for your community doesn't go unnoticed. You are outstanding, and I appreciate you and all that you do.

Most importantly, special thanks to you, my reader, for taking the time to read my books. I really hope you enjoyed this escape to Side Lake. Thank you for all your love and support. I appreciate all of you.